# A MAN IN PIECES

HENRY CORRIGAN

*Dedicated to my wife for keeping me in one piece, and to my daughter for being exactly who she is, rain or shine. I love you both. Always.*

Tom almost smiled, despite the pain.

Maybe it was how the kids laughed, or the way they moved, all flailing limbs and flapping jaws, their shrieks pealing across the street like remote controlled planes. There were four of them, all boys, and the tallest one, broad-faced with a nose like a putting wedge, dove headfirst into a snow drift before rolling easily to his feet. Every inch of him came up frosted, and his smile was as bright as the ice.

Two others, one thin and four-eyed, the other all braces and freckles, wordlessly dropped to their knees and started building a snowman together. The fourth, chubbiest by far, peeked sneakily from behind one of the cars in the driveway, a growing pile of snowballs at his feet.

With only one good hand and leg left to his name, Tom wobbled then hip checked the storm door open. He scowled at the flakes as they swept by. Light as confectioner's sugar and deceptive as hell; the kind of shit that should fall apart but would pull at your tires in every turn.

The cold put his teeth on edge as he hobbled out on his stoop. Too late; he realized he'd put his keys in his usual pocket. He held his lunch bag between hip and cast and contorted himself until his muscles strained painfully, but the keys came out before any other part of him gave in.

He locked the door behind him, turning just in time to see the door across the street burst open. Out of it bounded a little one, half the size of the rest, same nose, same broad face as the tall one, but she lacked his coordination, and her long dark hair flew behind her like a personal flag.

From his hiding place, Chubby watched her too, and Tom didn't find it hard to know what he was thinking. The minute she hit the snow she started running around the other three boys in chaotic circles. She wore a parka that was the pinkest thing Tom had ever seen in his life, and she chattered non-stop.

Chubby would peg her first, hard, and she'd probably cry and shriek, which would bring mommy out, but there was nothing for it. It was the way of boys and girls at that age. It's what Tom would have done if he'd been Chubby.

As if he was keeping to a script, Chubby ducked back down and mashed two snowballs together until he had a real bellringer in his hands. Tom saw him smile and straighten; his arm cocked back with all that flabby weight behind it.

A small, white missile caught him right in the eye.

Chubby yelped like a kicked dog. He wiped furiously at his face. Tom blinked and shook his head in surprise.

The kid sister was beaming like a spotlight, both arms high in a celebratory V. It took less than a second for the other boys to start the pointing and laughing. Chubby's face turned red, and Tom thought he saw the glint of tears, but that might've been the snow melting on his cheeks. Older brother gave kid sister a high five and then they went to help the others with their snowman.

Chubby and his stockpile were forgotten, and play resumed.

Tom glanced towards his car, which seemed a million miles away. The kids couldn't see how fast it was coming down, or how it was sticking to everything in sight. They wouldn't have to feel the ice beneath their tires and the ruts and the cracked roadways and the salt and sand so thick it could strip the paint off a car. The most they'd see of it would be watching their parents white knuckling the wheel.

Tom envied them for that. It had only been a couple hours since his last dose of pain meds but already he could feel it. His broken bits were starting to throb again, but it was a groggy kind of pain, almost slipshod, as if someone had laid a shawl across his shoulders that just happened to weigh forty pounds.

In the back of his mind he knew it was a risk heading out, even if he'd been a hundred percent. Already he anticipated the slip of the wheel and the stupid fucks out there driving like traction was something the other guy had to worry about.

*Nothing for it, troop. Get your ass in gear.*

The voice was right. He never called in yesterday and this was the wrong time to make a mistake like that. Who knew what Asshole Mike had been up to while he was gone? He couldn't afford to let that sonuvabitch get a foothold, not this close to the end. If he did...if management even thought it was a contest...

*Fuck it. Won't happen.*

So what if he hadn't called in? It was his first sick day in what, a year? Hell, longer than that, had to be. He didn't need to explain himself. He just had to walk in as he was.

*Hey guys! How's it going? Oh this? Yeah, it was nothing. Had an accident yesterday, but I'm here now. No big deal. Why am I not home, Pat? Come on, man. Got work to do, don't I?*

Nodding to himself, Tom pulled up the collar of his jacket, took a step down the walk, and almost had his feet shoot out from under him.

He teetered and staggered, nearly fell, managed to get his balance but at the cost of his bad foot hitting the ground hard. The bones twisted and howled, sending tracer rounds of pain across his whole body. Tom cursed loudly and sucked in a great big mouthful of burning winter air and then he was hacking like he'd never stop. He coughed 'til his chest burned, 'til his eyes watered, like there was something wet and sickly inside him he couldn't get out.

He ended up bent over double with a bitter taste in the back of his throat. He breathed as deep and slow as he could 'til his heart stopped its panicky scramble, and he could see straight again. Straightening slowly, he filled his mouth with all that gunk, and spat it, long and wet, into the snow.

Being sure to keep his head high, he turned towards the kids, a hard glare ready for any of them stupid enough to be staring. But the effort was wasted. None of them noticed. Chubby had rejoined the ranks and their play had evolved into a bastardization of football and dodgeball, one kid tasked with making it to the curb before the others pelted the living hell out of him.

Tom wiped his chin and thought about the drive ahead. It would be a bitch, no doubt, but if he got his ass in gear, he could still make it with time to spare. That was all he needed, really. Just enough to fend off Asshole Mike and prove that he deserved to be there.

Stepping carefully, limping heavily, he inched his way down the walk. He'd forgotten his gloves inside, so by the time he cleared the headlights and all the windows, his hands were as white as porcelain and ready to crack.

It took more maneuvering but eventually he opened the door, and his ass met the front seat. As soon as the Crown Vic barked to life, Tom cranked the heater as high as it would go. He couldn't afford to give it any warmup time, but he forced himself to sit there for a couple minutes anyway. The Vic was ten years old and not in the best of shape. Stressing it, even a little bit, in the middle of winter, was a bad idea. He stared at the dashboard clock as the seconds passed. The clenching in his gut, the way his skin and bones and fucking everything itched to get moving, made it seem like the seconds were taking their time. Out for a stroll through a warm and sunny park Tom would never find.

He closed his eyes and sucked in one long breath, hoping it would steady him, but before he could get that far, the hacking came back, stealing away what little breath he had.

This coughing fit hurt even worse than the last, and when all that wet filled his mouth again, he rolled down the window and hocked it into the snow. By the time he looked back at the dash, the last minute had passed. He threw the car in gear and peeled out of the drive. The kids didn't notice his passing and he paid them no mind. He was too busy praying for a break in the lights.

Out in the street, he twisted the wheel, and headed for the main road. As he picked up speed, the wind stripped away everything he was too weak to reach - the icicles off his bumpers, the slush off the wheels, even the little bit of red off the door, the thin, drooling streak that stretched from the window to halfway down the paint. It slipped away unnoticed in the gray and white morning.

Sunday January 17, 2016

January was a murderer, as Mike's mother used to say.

It didn't simply end each day. It killed them remorselessly; gone too soon, and with so much still to do.

The sunlight was nearly dead as Mike pulled the Explorer up the drive. He grabbed the grocery bag out of the backseat, he popped the door, muscles already tense against the cold. Before he cut the engine, the readout on his dash called it eight degrees outside. The air was as motionless as a mannequin, but even without it, the night wrapped its arms around him and scooped the breath out of his lungs.

He hunched his shoulders and ran past his wife's Corolla and was still frozen by the time he slipped the key in the lock. Clack, push, scrape and he was in the warmth of the house. January's crushing arms walked in with him but faded quickly as he stood there.

"Hello!" he called, kicking the door closed behind him.

"Hey, babe!" Claire's reply was muted, distant, propelled from deep in the house.

The front door opened into a carpeted living room, white walls, a cushioned L-shaped couch, flat screen TV in the corner by the window. Mike stripped off his coat and draped it over the padded easy chair, a colorful strip of cloth crammed into one of the creases catching his eye.

He plucked it out and stared at a familiar, woollen patch of red and green, the needles hanging off the ends like a half-assed wind chime. He rolled the whole thing up along with the remaining, apple-sized ball of wool and stuffed it in his pocket and headed down the hall. He found Claire at the kitchen sink, sponge in hand, soap past her wrists. Her smile was worn at the edges.

"Hey, handsome. Thanks again. I'm sorry."

They'd painted the kitchen a summer yellow last year, and depending on where she stood, the halo of bright color around Claire's black hair reminded him of sunflowers. He crossed the distance between them and kissed her, the touch of her lips loosening a couple of knots in his chest.

"Don't worry about it, beautiful."

"I can't believe I forgot we were out of mayo. I'm so sorry."

Mike cracked the seal on the jar. "Oh, would you stop? I told you it's no big deal."

"Yes, it is. But thank you for being kind."

He shook his head but decided to move on. "How're the two of you doing?"

He laid a hand on her stomach and felt the cooling dampness of dishwater. Claire put her hand over his and kissed him again.

"We're fine. He's been helping me clean up what remains of lunch."

"Oh yeah? How'd he do that?"

"By not kicking or giving mommy cramps for a couple hours so she can actually *wash* the dishes."

Mike chuckled and pulled her in against his side. "Glad to hear it. Thanks for helping out, Tim." He drummed his fingers lightly across Claire's stomach.

"Oh!" Claire jumped and held his hand in place.

A moment later he felt the kick of a tiny foot against his palm. He laughed and kissed Claire's cheek. "He's getting impatient."

"He's not the only one. And we are not naming him Tim."

"It's my dad's name."

"His middle name. And it stinks, no offense to your dad. Everybody will call him Timmy. I've watched way too much South Park for that to be cute."

Mike leaned against the counter and shook his head. "Here we go. What do you want to name him?"

"You know me, I'm old fashioned. I want something classic, like Gabriel."

Mike made a point of staring at her like she'd suddenly turned purple. "Timmy you don't want. But you're okay with Gabe?"

"No one's going to call him that."

"Well no one's going to call him Gabriel either so what does that leave him with? 'Hey, you?'"

She splashed him. "Gabriel's a great name. People will respect it."

"You mean the same way everybody called your grandfather Zeke, instead of Ezekiel?"

She picked up the sponge and held it on him like a nickel plated .45. "Do not make fun of my Grampa."

Mike raised his hands high. "Anything you say, Crazy Lady."

The corners of Claire's mouth ratcheted up a couple of degrees. She gestured towards the table with the sponge. "Good. Now sit down. Dinner will be just a few more minutes."

Mike dropped his hands and gave his wife an exasperated look. "Babe, you know you don't have to keep making dinner. You're supposed to be resting. *I* can make dinner sometimes."

Claire didn't look up from the glass in her hand. "You've been working all day. I've been home. I needed something to do."

"I thought that's what this was for." He pulled the knitting out of his pocket and waggled it.

Claire groaned and put the last fork in the rack to dry. "I can't spend the next month and a half sitting on my ass and knitting, I'm not a housewife from the 50s. Plus, I'm...Well, I'm not that great at it."

"Oh, please babe. I'm sure it'll be cute once you finish it. It's gonna be a sweater, right?"

"It's supposed to be booties."

Mike looked at the piece of stitching again. It was an oblong rectangle, and the colors were so haphazard they all but bled into each other. He looked at his wife.

The sponge came out again and Claire smiled like a serial killer. "If you value your life, I'd advise you not to say anything right now."

Mike smiled back. "I don't have to say anything. The whole thing kind of...You know, speaks for itself."

Several minutes were lost as Claire chased her husband around the kitchen. Mike, arms up, palms out, did his best to shield himself from her fury but the fact that he was laughing his head off did little to help him. Eventually, both out of breath and with smiles that made their jaws ache, they settled into their usual seats at their white, art deco dinner table.

They held hands and were, for the moment, content to sit quietly together in that time before 'How was your day?' and 'How are you feeling?'

Mike ran his thumb across the backs of Claire's knuckles and looked out the window. It may have been cold as hell, but it was beautiful too. Cloudless, bright with stars and what he used to call a fingernail moon when he was a kid.

All the peacefulness that permeated these quiet seconds didn't completely unravel the rocks in his stomach, but it helped him breathe better. He glanced at his wife and noted the resigned sadness that pulled at her mouth. He didn't need to ask what she was thinking. He followed her gaze to the empty clay pots and rows of faded signs. The garden had been their first big project the summer they moved in six years ago.

He lifted her hand and kissed her fingertips. "We'll bring it back in the spring, Love. Don't worry."

She half smiled and squeezed his hand. "I know. It's just not right. No tomatoes, no fresh veggies. All of it gone to the weeds and squirrels."

Their backyard was tiny by most people's standards, but what they had they'd put to good use. Off to one side was a stretch of tilled earth hemmed in by lumber and long, neat planting rows. From the way Claire told it, there'd always been a garden in her family. Mother, Grandmother, Great Grandmother. Her earliest memories were of munching mint leaves and her mother wiping the juice of cherry tomatoes off her chin.

Mike, a dyed-in-the-wool meat and potatoes man who'd never met a salad he trusted, found himself in his late twenties falling in love with fresh cucumbers and homemade salad dressing, and with the beautiful woman who made them.

He thought about those days and couldn't stop himself from feeling sad about the harvest this year. Claire's pregnancy had been hard, not only putting her on bed rest, but leaving her physically drained most days. The weather had been no help either. Spring was late getting to its feet, leaving the growth and warmth stymied by a winter which not only pummeled everything, but landed several hard shots long after the bell, too.

Dry, brown and cracked, the ground looked like nothing so much as mistreated leather. The makeshift stalks they'd driven in to help keep the plants upright now looked like stick figures frozen in place, immobile until spring thawed them out.

Mike cobbled together his best smile and aimed it at Claire. "It'll all bounce right back, Love. You'll see. All it needs is some warm weather and attention. Come spring we'll have a baby *and* a bushel of tomatoes. It'll be a toss-up as to which one is redder, the kid or the fruit."

The look she gave him. He'd never know if she truly believed him, or just chose to buy it.

"Yeah, you're right," she said, giving him that half smile again, only with half as much conviction. Her chin came to rest in her hand, and she stared not out at the garden but at some unknowable spot in the geography of the table.

One of the rocks in Mike's stomach, one of the big ones, had jagged edges. "What is it, babe? What's wrong?"

She looked at him sideways and he knew what it was before she'd even spoken.

"When do you think we'll hear from Jerry?"

"I'm not sure, Love." Mike tried for calm indifference, but his mouth didn't seem to want to form the words right. "I was thinking about giving him a call tomorrow. But he said he probably wouldn't hear anything 'til Thursday, so..."

"I know. I can't help worrying about it though."

"Me neither."

"We got another letter from the oil company today."

"Ugh, hell. Okay, lay it on me."

"No, no. It's not bad news. They said we qualified for the payment plan. Two hundred and fifty a month instead of six hundred dropped on us all at once."

"Thank God. That bill always put my teeth on edge every time I saw it."

"Huh. I'll see your teeth and I'll raise you a blinding headache over the mortgage."

Mike groaned and, of all things, that finally got her to laugh. The sound had a touch of exhaustion to it and a splash of bitterness, but underneath was a sweetness that made Mike pick up his head.

Claire put her arms around him and kissed his cheek. The timer went off on the stove and she wobbled over to take the lid off something steaming. "Oh, hey. I almost forgot. I got an email from an old coworker earlier."

Mike looked up. "Oh yeah? What about?"

"She wanted to know if I had any poster boards she could use. Her class has a big science project coming up and she doesn't have any room in the budget for more."

Mike sat very still, hoping if he gave it a minute that sentence would make more sense.

Claire snickered. "That's just what I was thinking! I couldn't believe she asked me!"

"What did you say?"

"I told her I threw out all of my school supplies after I left."

"Okay. But what about all of your stuff up in the—"

"Shut up. Listen," Claire said, excitedly patting the air. "She said it's terrible there now. Thirty-five kids to a class *and no aid!* You should've heard her on the phone. She sounded like she was ready to pull her hair out and strangle somebody with it."

Mike laughed and shrugged. "Well then, they shouldn't have fired you if they're that shorthanded."

"I know, but I wasn't the only one they booted. People with a lot more seniority had to leave too."

"Yeah, but three years should count for something."

"Not in catholic school, babe, I'm sorry to say."

That worried look was starting to entrench itself into her features again so Mike, desperate to cut it off, reached out and took her hand. He laid his lips against each knuckle until she smirked. "We're going to be okay."

"Sure, I guess," she said with more hope and surety.

Mike kept pecking. "The garden will come back; you'll get a new job, and we'll have a kid we probably won't screw up too much."

She smiled for real this time, at last. She kissed him and pressed her cheek against his, a motion of comfort older than human beings.

Dinner was simple in the best of ways. Thick slices of rye bread with tuna fish slathered between, bowls of steaming chicken stew, a chilled bottle of beer for him, ice water for her. The kind of no-frills meal you need on a winter night. They ate in an easy quiet, broken only by tales of his day at the office, her day of trying not to lose her mind to boredom.

Afterward, Mike slid his chair over and put his arm around her. She watched the sky this time while he sat, eyes half closed, just breathing in the soap and shampoo scent of her. She wore a simple housedress, room enough to accommodate her belly, but so deep a green it showcased her hair and the spattering of freckles at her neck. It took some twisting, but he managed to touch his lips to her skin in that no man's land between neck and shoulder.

"Mmm," she sighed.

With the expanse of his son, the hemline of Claire's dress gave ground to the point that when she crossed her legs, it pulled back above mid-thigh. His wife's legs were pure cream, and her skin showing the rarest of genetics which never tanned, only burned. When he turned his head just a hair, Mike was treated to the sight of her bra, white as spun cotton, through the scoop neck of the dress.

He could tell by her inattention that she hadn't noticed. She sat calmly, head at an angle as she lost herself in the sky. Meanwhile, Mike studied the curve of her breast. Pale as the rest of her, he knew its texture as well as his own skin. Without orders, his brain passed on communications, memories, that reminded him of how heavy and soft they were, how they filled his whole hand with a warm, inviting texture.

He remembered an early morning, one where even the alarm clock was still asleep, her soft kisses on the back of his neck, waking him, her warm hands turning him onto his back, the sudden feel of her skin, his nerves jerking alive at her already naked form as she straddled him, how she sat back and put his hands on her breasts, made him keep them there as she rode him.

The memories were clear, but like a compressed file, the effect lost in the recording. Mike shifted in his seat, caught between an oppressive need to overwrite the file, and a logical voice scolding him for it. He couldn't, not shouldn't, but *couldn't*, and God damn it to hell.

There was a tingling in his fingers and a hard, frustrated ache between his legs, a withdrawal symptom from the feel of her skin. It had been months. Mike tried to breathe slowly and stare at nothing, to give it all time to subside.

Claire turned to him. "Sorry, babe," she grimaced. "But my back has run out of things to say to this chair."

Mike smiled and helped her up. "I'm sure it won't mind if you go talk to the couch for a while."

Claire nodded. "That's a good idea. The couch likes me. We get along so well."

She kissed him the way long couples do, quickly, but with deep affection. He blinked and took a snapshot of her as she walked away. There was a pronounced sway to her hips he knew was all his son. As she rounded the corner he smiled, the urge he'd felt before had subsided, but with it came a different kind of ache. His lower back was sore, and his neck creaked with every turn. He closed his eyes and dug his knuckles in until the burn of being open for too long went away.

Another minute of sitting, of finally getting his neck to crack and that was enough. He took a deep breath and then set to the dishes.

---

Claire's hips always hurt, no matter what she did. Sitting, standing, grinding her knuckles into her spine 'til she bit her lip...none of it helped; it just created gradations of pain. Last month she'd established a beachhead in the junction of their couch; three pillows, an afghan for her legs, a rickety TV tray with remote, heating pad and cordless phone. She settled into it and groaned. The pain smoothed out to a manageable ripple.

Quietly, she prayed. *Dear bladder. Please don't make me have to get up again for the next thirty to forty-five minutes.*

From the kitchen came the splash of running water and the light, *squee-squee* of a sponge. Claire looked towards it and rubbed her left wrist, a guilty tell that had been with her since she was seven.

"Thanks, babe," she called.

"Not a problem."

"I'm sorry I can't help." She heard him snort. The sound he reserved for when he thought she was being silly.

"Don't worry about it."

He said that every day now.

Mutely, she sighed and shook her head. With so much time on her hands, there was nothing to do but watch TV and worry. She felt ashamed of the next thought, but it was too true to push aside. *Christ, he looks terrible.*

He walked like she did, slow and careful, no wasted energy. His skin was drained of its natural color while his eyes, normally a sharp, playful brown, were tinged with red. He looked as if even *he* didn't know what was keeping him going and it was tough to deal with that herself. But seeing it on him...Well, she didn't know. It was right up there in the top three things she knew were out of whack.

Some days, the memory felt fifty years old and dusty as an old book, others, it was as perfect and firm as fresh lemons. But either way, Claire never forgot the night Mike brought her home to meet his parents. They hadn't even been dating three months, but even then, at the beginning, she knew this was different.

Relationships are like anything homegrown. Some are messy and fun and then gone for the season. Others start off sweet but end bitter. And a rare few, if you do it up right, dig deep and stay with you.

She'd never really gotten the chance to meet Mike's mother. On their first date, all Mike had said was that she was ill, and Claire thought he secretly appreciated her decision not to press.

It wasn't until two months in, both cuddled up on the couch, that she learned how deep his fears for his mom went. A commercial for some new cancer drug came on the TV, one where it took the voice-over longer to get through the side-effects than to explain what the drug was for. By the end of it, Mike had grown very quiet, the set lines of his face making him look older, more worn than only a minute ago. She asked him, and eventually the answer came in bits and pieces, parceled out between shrugs meant to tell her he was okay, it was covered.

It was his father who finally decided they should meet, though she was never quite sure how she knew. Mike just told her all of a sudden. They needed to have dinner.

"Claire! It's so nice to finally meet you." Edmund was his name. Claire was a sucker for anything old fashioned.

"Thank you so much for inviting me."

She was barely able to hide her shock before she smiled and kissed his cheek. She just hadn't expected him to look so *old*. The moment they met, she thought of Charles Holloway, Bradbury's regretful librarian with moon white hair, a man in his sixties who looked twenty years older.

He brushed her thanks away, a mannerism she'd seen reflected in his son a hundred times. "Oh, it's no trouble. I've been wanting to meet the girl who turned my son's head."

Mike flushed at that one, and Claire giggled. She teased him about that for months afterward.

They sat together, three at a four-person table. The meal, as she'd come to think of it, was much like the family; simple and fine. They had thick cut pork chops, mashed potatoes, homemade brown gravy, grilled asparagus, beer and a bottle of Cab.

Both men drank beer and, when seated side by side, they looked like a time lapse photo of the same face. They shrugged and smiled in smooth, easy ways and told stories with a natural rhythm.

Back then she'd been new. She couldn't ask, not about the smell of sickness, subtle but constant. It permeated even the scent of the chops grilling on the stove and Edmund's aftershave. It emanated strongest from a short hallway just off the living room. Both men avoided looking at it, and the closed door at its end. There'd been a moment, halfway through the meal, all of them with glasses tipped to their lips when a sound intruded; a wet burst of coughing, heavy but brief. It lasted only a few seconds, but the two men froze all the same. They stopped, not blinking, not even breathing for those seconds. When it passed and did not repeat, they came alive again.

The closest she came to asking was much later, after dinner, with Edmund clearing the dishes. "Is there anything I can do to help?"

"Oh, thank you, but no. I can clean up my own mess."

"Are you sure?"

He'd looked at her and very slowly smiled. In the small space between them she knew he understood what she really meant. Claire had no idea what she could have done to be of help. Probably nothing, but that wasn't what mattered to him. Edmund's smile deepened the lines around his eyes 'til they branched out like a map of long dried riverbeds.

"Yeah. You're one of the real sweethearts. Thanks again but..." He put his back to her and busied himself at the sink. "Don't worry about it."

The reflection of that night was in the clatter of the dishes in the next room. She wanted to tell Mike to stop, but the truth wasn't easy to live with.

She needed him too badly.

The bills were a constant problem, the housework never stopped, and they had no one else to rely on. Neither of them had brothers or sisters, and both sets of parents were dead more than a decade. She flashed again on Edmund's face and saw that haggard look which said he was breaking down by inches but would never ask for help.

She'd never understood why, but it was part of what made her fall in love with Mike. That willingness to shoulder more than he could handle because he was needed. But...

Half an hour later, after she heard the last dish being put away, he came in and sat next to her. He sighed deeply, eyes half closed, head at an angle that said sleep would take him by the throat soon.

"I love you, babe," he said. The kiss he planted on her cheek was sweetened by beer. A glass each night she'd never begrudge him, no matter how much a glass of white wine would have meant to her.

"I love you too," she said. They leaned on each other like walking sticks as they made their way to bed.

Tom took a sip of whiskey. "You're a fucking moron."

"Seriously brother? I tell you I'm thinking about getting a divorce and *that's* all you can say to me?"

Another sip, and Tom smirked at his friend. "Yeah, cause it's all I need to say to you."

Corley's Bar and Grill was as stripped down as a bar could get, which was how Tom preferred it. Finding one that wasn't festooned with televisions was rare, but so was finding one that turned a blind eye to regulars wanting to use the old smoking shelter out back. Tom counted himself lucky for stumbling on it a few years ago.

"Come on, man. I gotta do this," Jimmy all but whined.

"That a fact? Tell me why."

He and Jimmy Timmons, his best friend, occupied a pair of stools at the corner by the door. Behind Jimmy's head was the main window so every time Tom gave him his best 'You're full of shit' glare, he couldn't help but look outside.

"Look, things between Lisa and me are just...it's just not there, you know what I mean? It's not fun anymore. We've been married for thirty fucking years. Every morning I wake up and all I can think is *Ugh, you again?* It's just...Fuck it, brother, time for something new."

Jimmy threw back his head and drained his beer. He held up a finger to Marcie, the bartender, who dutifully smiled and brought him another. Tom shook his head.

"Look, if you're going to pester me with this bullshit, can you at least not drink cheap shit while you're doing it? Since when did you pussy out and switch to beer?"

"What? It's nothing. I just, you know. I was looking at the bills last month and thought...Well, I mean, if I'm really gonna do this, then maybe it'd be smart to save some money."

Tom blinked like he'd been slapped. Jimmy telling him he was thinking about leaving Lisa was dumb but not unexpected. Those two were a fucking case study in Staying Together Out of Complacency. But hearing his friend talk about money made him think that it was twelve bucks a whiskey to four for a beer and they were both already on their third round, which led to Tom thinking about his wife and what he had in his wallet and what he had in the bank and none of those were things he wanted to fucking think about right then, so...

He bonked the side of his head with his palm and pointedly looked past his friend. "You want to talk about saving money? How about you get rid of that gas guzzler of yours?"

Out in the parking lot, Jimmy's Dodge Ram dwarfed the cars on either side of it. The vanity plate read LAWNMAN, and beneath that, a novelty pair of testicles swung from the trailer hitch.

Jimmy looked embarrassed but stuck to his beer. "Is this how the night's gonna go? With you giving me shit 'til I either have to kill you or call a cab?"

Tom started to laugh but, all of a sudden, he didn't have the breath to keep going. A strong itch took over his throat and his chest tightened, as if someone were standing behind him with a strap belted around his middle. He looked away from Jimmy quickly and fumbled in his jacket like he was looking for his pack. Another good thing about Corley's. The music was loud enough to cover his coughing fit.

"Come on. I need a smoke," he said, once the strap eased up a notch.

He stood up and headed for the back, only stopping when he realized Jimmy wasn't right behind him. He looked back.

"What? You going to drink shitty beer *and* leave me to stand outside by myself? That ain't right."

With another moment's hesitation his friend followed, and they both stood stomping their feet in a lean-to that smelled of decades of stale, gray smoke. Around them the traffic burred like a mile-wide white noise machine.

"Okay, so tell me. What's the plan?"

Jimmy took a drag off the red Tom had given him. "What do you mean 'what's my plan?'"

"I mean, you and Lisa. Where are you going from here? What's next?"

"Next...I tell Lisa it's over. There's no sense in being mean about it. She doesn't need to leave. I'll find a place of my own and then..."

"On to something new?" Tom asked, mocking.

"Look, what the hell is your problem? You been married just as long as I have!"

"Longer. Coming up on thirty-four years pretty soon, I think."

"Right, right! And you can't tell me you don't think about being a bachelor again."

"Of course I do, dumbass."

"Well then, how come you're not on my side?" Jimmy whined.

"Cause I still remember what you were like when you were single."

"The hell you talking about? I had a great time getting home and having nobody to take care of. Going anywhere I liked and never having to check in. And the girls? Shiiiiit."

The lean-to wasn't well lit, but Tom could still make out how hard the beer was working on his friend. Jimmy was a Polack through and through with skin that, on a good day, a poet might've called florid or ruddy. But when he'd been drinking there wasn't any other description for it but beef-steak red. It was an unsightly thing to see on a creature not meant to end up on a grill.

Tom pulled in the last drag and held it. For a second, he felt lightheaded, but thankfully it passed. Twin plumes left his nose as he ground the butt beneath his boot. "Okay, that's about enough."

"What's wrong?" Jimmy asked.

Tom shouldered his way back into the bar, hearing Jimmy right on his heels. Back at his stool he polished off his whiskey and signaled for another. Jimmy looked him over anxiously.

Tom could feel how much his friend wanted him to approve his plan.

"Come on, brother. What's the matter?"

Tom shrugged. "Nothing. But can I just say, I'm sorry. I mean, I really had no idea I was sitting here with Don Draper. Can you believe that?"

"Fuck you."

"No, I mean it! I didn't recognize you. Maybe it was the comb-over."

"Fuck you!"

"Or the love handles."

"You prick!"

"Cause I gotta say, they look great on you. Where can I get a pair of those?"

"Fuck. You. *Hard!*"

"Look man, do you want my help or not?" Tom pressed, genuinely hoping to impart some wisdom.

"Not, asshole," grumbled Jimmy.

"Well, you're getting it anyway. And I'm gonna start with this—bachelor life sucks. Yours sucked more than most."

"Go to hell!"

Jimmy made to stand, but the beer had too good a grip on him. He lost his balance and nearly fell backward off his stool. Tom caught his arm, steadied him, and then held up three fingers close to his face.

"One. You probably don't want to remember this, but before you met Lisa, you had a dry spell that lasted more than a year, and that was back when you still had prospects. And hair."

"You son of a bitch."

"Two. The breadwinner in your family is Lisa, not you. She handles all of the accounts; she knows where everything is, which means the minute you walk out on her, you're fucked."

"It won't be that bad."

Tom held up his remaining finger, smiling, as he'd saved the best for last. "Three. If you're here with me, just *thinking* about getting a divorce, that means Lisa is days away from serving you papers."

"What?"

"Think about it. You said you wake up feeling sick of looking at her, right? Well, to me, that means Lisa not only knows what you're thinking, but is probably thinking the same thing, only she's smart enough not to let on. And if you're just now telling me you're bored, then you can guaran-fucking-tee that Lisa has been complaining to her friends about you for months."

Tom watched his friend closely. He was staring blankly at the bottles behind the bar, his hands shook, and he was sweating like fucking mad. He gave the impression he'd be turning pale if it weren't for the beer in his system. Sensing it was time for the final charge, Tom put a hand on Jimmy's shoulder.

"Look, if you don't want to end up spending the rest of your life failing to get girls to fuck you in whatever shitty little apartment you end up in after Lisa boots you out, then I strongly fucking suggest you go home and do everything you can to prove to her you're not a complete asshole."

Jimmy went silent for a long minute.

Though Tom regretted being so harsh, he never let it stop him. He came from a military family, with uncles in every branch of the service. He practically had a genetic predisposition for being cruel to be kind. No sense in sprinkling sugar; it never helped nobody anyway.

"Why the fuck am I friends with you?" Jimmy asked finally.

Tom couldn't hear any hate in it, just a lot of hard truth. He sniggered.

"Same reason I'm friends with you. And look at it this way, I saved you a couple hundred bucks on a lawyer."

Jimmy made to chug his beer but stopped before the bottle touched his lips. Setting it down, he waved at Marcie. "Can I get a whiskey over here, honey?"

"There you fucking go!" Tom slapped his friend's back and, flicking a switch on his own worries, ordered another for himself.

*Beep-beep, beep-beep, beep-beep, beep-beep, beep-beep, beep-beep, beep-beep...*

With his eyes closed, Mike blearily reached out and prodded the alarm clock.

*...beep-beep, beep-beep, beep-beep, beep-beep, beep-beep...*

Groaning, he groped across the top of the machine and just started punching buttons.

*...beep-beep-beep, beep-beep-beep, beep-beep-beep-, beep-beep-beep, beep-beep-beep, beep-beep-beep-beep-beep-beep-beep...*

He slammed his fist down like a club and miraculously the beeping stopped. Next to him, Claire mumbled.

"M-Mike?"

"I'm here, love," he said, voice as thick as the mattress.

"What was 'at?"

"Alarm clock," he said, throwing an arm over his wife, squeezing her tight.

She grunted. Her words came out in a slow, sloppy way. "What happened to music? Thought you had your thing 'nnected to-it."

He glanced back over his shoulder. The iPod was sticking straight up out of the docking port. "I did. Sorry, love."

"Mmmm." She snuggled closer against him, kissed his forearm where it lay close to her cheek.

Mike squeezed her tight again and kissed the back of her head. Her black hair, this close to his face, was the color of good dark chocolate. It smelled of oranges and lavender.

He trailed one hand down 'til it came to rest on her swollen belly. Smiling, he breathed in the scent of her hair. Below, just where his palm lay, he felt a tiny kick, mirrored a second later by his wife's own foot skirting along the sheet, mother and son acting together like a knee tapped for reflexes.

Mike smiled and had a prayer already in mind, one asking to let them stay like this as long as possible, but his eyes wouldn't allow it. They remained tense and implacable, finally pulling his gaze toward the clock again.

It was twenty to seven. He had to get up and hop into the shower *now*.

Leaning up on an elbow, he kissed her cheek. "Love you."

"'ve you."

He slid out of bed as quietly as he could. His robe hung on the corner of the door, and he grabbed it as he swept past. Twenty minutes later he left the light off as he headed back into the bedroom, robe open down to his hips, still radiating heat from the shower. He knew the room by muscle memory. Socks, underwear, shirt and pants were all grabbed by texture which somehow always managed to be okay together when the lights came on.

He'd packed his lunch the night before, so he had an extra minute to lean in and...

Lips pressed against a cheek. Another on the forehead just below the hairline. She never so much as stirred.

"See you tonight, love," he said.

The 'Nnnmmm' came just as he closed the door behind him.

Work was thirty minutes away, forty with traffic. That good feeling, the one which had felt embedded in his skin, lasted right up until he pulled into the parking lot.


"Morning, Sarah. Morning, Alma. Morning, asshole."

Mike kept his mouth shut as Tom Downes, the lead coordinator in their section, strode into the office, smiling. His lunch bag swung loosely at his side, and he had a cigarette tucked behind one ear.

"How are the natives? They restless yet?"

Sarah spoke without looking up. "Haven't seen anybody, but I'm sure they'll be here soon, banging on the door."

Tom tucked his ample stomach behind Lauren's unoccupied desk. "That's the fuckin' truth. Banging like they're —" He started to cough. "Like they want us to...To be their—"

The cough became a wet, sickening hack. Tom pounded his chest, eyes tearing and his face turning purple. Mike tried to concentrate on his screen, but it was impossible to ignore the noise. A few seconds later Tom finally ducked under the desk and expelled something into the trash can that sounded as if it had congealed within his chest days ago. It wasn't 'til Tom straightened up again that Mike realized he was the only one still watching.

"Hey, asshole," Tom croaked, eyes as coarse as gravel. "Since you're staring at me so close, I guess that means you've finished reorganizing that spreadsheet I gave you."

Mike had the urge to close his eyes and rub his temples, but instead he shrugged. "You only gave it to me yesterday, *five minutes* before we left for the day."

"That a fact? Funny, 'cause that's not the way I remember it."

Tom wore a smirk Mike knew so well he cringed inside the moment he saw it. He could feel everyone else in the office looking at them the way speeding drivers will stare at car accidents.

"See, I remember telling you it was important, and that Patrick would need it for his meeting at one. So I don't know about you, but I think that means a guy shouldn't sit around wasting any more time by arguing with me like an asshole."

"I'm not wasting—"

"And come to think of it, you know what else I remember? I remember giving you that spreadsheet *twenty* minutes before we left."

Mike's skin burned. His left leg bounced incessantly, and he was hyperaware of the way his collar scratched against his neck. "Do you actually think that makes a difference?"

"You tell me. After all, you're the one saying that five minutes and twenty are the same thing."

There was so much disgust in Mike's body, he could taste it in the back of his throat. If he could have, he would have spat every drop of it into Tom's smirking, hateful mouth.

"Come on, Mike. Tell me, was it twenty minutes or just five?"

Mike clenched his jaw 'til his skull ached.

"Five and twenty don't sound the same to me," Tom persisted. "They sound the same to you, Margaret?"

Margaret was a blonde, kind, vaguely egg-shaped woman with two grown sons and enough brains to pretend that Tom didn't exist.

"Margaret? Margaret, you with us? You're reminding me of my wife right now. Don't make a peep until I forget to take out the garbage."

Mike couldn't take it. "Okay, fine, Tom. Fine. It was twenty minutes, not five. But I still don't see how that makes any—"

"*What you don't see,* buddy, is all the time you've wasted being an asshole. So how about you stop mouthing off to me and pretend like you give a shit about your fucking job, okay? The spreadsheet's due at one, and the clock's ticking."

They locked eyes and it could have been a second, or a minute, but it didn't matter because all Mike cared about was the shame he felt when he looked away first. He saw Tom swagger his way down the hall and flipping off his retreating back was like eating one tasteless potato chip. Nowhere near satisfying.

Tom's door slammed and the office died. At least, that was how it seemed. Like it had been heavily pregnant, ready to pop, but died tragically in childbirth. From instep to crown, bone to bile, Mike wanted to swivel around in his chair and scream.

*What the fuck, guys!? My days aren't hard enough?*

He kept his peace, but it was a near thing. He'd almost have laughed if it wasn't so goddamn sad. Asshole was his nickname now, had been for months. It was how Tom addressed him ever since he became lead and no one, not even management, said boo about it.

Cursing under his breath, Mike regretted ever taking this job, not because it was a bad choice, but because it had been the only one available at the time. As with most third-party insurance companies, Cynagin's clients were largely retired roofers, housepainters and plumbers—self-employed folks on fixed incomes who, due to the failures of old age, needed help paying for everything Medicare wouldn't cover.

Policy demanded that employees be 'cheery and aggressively helpful' when it came to their clients. However, that helpfulness was nowhere to be found whenever said employee needed something from management.

After his old job had downsized, Mike was left scrambling. Cynagin wasn't just the only company offering comparable benefits, it was the only company to call him back. With no other options and a pregnant wife needing to go out on FMLA, he'd considered himself so lucky to land this job he'd actually whooped when he got the call. Now...

Not even a minute after his time on the shaming rack, Alma stood up and pulled a long black remote from her top desk drawer. In the waiting area across from their desks, an off-brand flat screen shrieked to life, the competitive volume a consequence of their normal day. Between shouting clients, ringing phones, and the constant clicking of keys, the TV was cranked at all times.

Every one of them twitched as News 12 came on in its usual bright blue, self-importance. Front and center, an attractive blonde woman in her mid-thirties wore a polished smile, and a dark gray suit, and pointed at a garishly pixelated calendar.

*Happy Monday morning, Long Island. I'm Marissa Scott for Channel 12 News, and this is the forecast for the coming week.*

*Today is going to be clear but frigid with sunny skies and a high of about twenty-five. Tonight will be windy, with temperatures dropping into the teens again.*

*Unfortunately, it's only going to get worse from here on out. As you can see, all the way into Thursday we won't even crack twenty degrees and our weather center is tracking that cold front which has been wreaking havoc in the Midwest. We could see temperatures in the single digits by Friday morning and the first major snowstorm of the winter as well. As of now, forecasters are calling for at least a foot of snow, possibly even eighteen inches, so be sure to stock the fridge and get ready to break out those shovels.*

*That's the weather for you right now, but we'll have up to the minute forecasts for you throughout the rest of the week.*

Out of the corner of his eye, Mike saw Sarah shake her head.

"Oh, please, don't let it snow Friday."

"Why not?" Alma asked with her feet up on a chair and a pile of file folders in her lap. "We might get out early. Be a nice way to start the weekend."

Sarah planted her hands on her hips and stared morosely at the screen. Her eyes were narrow and the corners of her mouth tightly pinched. "They won't let us out for anything less than a blizzard. And even if they did, we'll have to spend twenty minutes cleaning off our cars, then an hour driving home, slipping and sliding the whole way. Besides, my daughter is supposed to go back to school Friday. If we get snowed in, I'll be stuck with her 'til Monday."

"I thought you liked having your daughter home."

"I do, but every time she comes home my laundry triples. You have no idea! That girl goes through clothes like...like...I don't even know. I just don't want any more dirty socks on my floor this weekend."

"Don't worry," Mike was shocked to hear himself say. "It won't be that bad."

Sarah sat down at her desk with a plunk. "Yes, it will. You remember the winter we had a couple years ago? That's what we're in for this year. A snowstorm every weekend for a month."

"Ugh, God yeah, I remember that," Margaret chimed in. "One night I had some friends over for dinner. They parked in the street and when I looked out my front window, I couldn't even see their car, the drifts were so high."

"I knew I should have picked up a snow-blower when they were on sale. My back can't take two feet of snow."

Mike did his best to tune them out. The job was soul-sucking anyway, but Sarah's negativity only made it worse. She complained at any given opportunity, her predictions pessimistic without fail, and when any new problems came up, she'd become infected with a loud, grating whine that could be heard clear across the office.

Mike stood up without warning, and cut through the prattle like an axe. He looked at his coworkers and they at him, their mouths slack, bodies tense, unaware of how frightened they looked at what he might say.

"I'm going for a walk."

All three visibly relaxed.

"No problem, we understand. Take your time, we got you

covered." For as much as Sarah could talk, Alma was always the first with a remark.

"Thanks." Mike grabbed his coat and headed for the fire stairs at the back of the office. The little alcove outside was used as an unofficial smoking shelter, but thankfully the wind kicked up, dragging the stench of stale cigarettes away.

The cold flooded through him, washing away all the hot dust in his head. With it gone, the thought came to give Chris another call. His friend was the only good line he had in the water for a new job, but it provided enough hope to keep him going. Mike had just started to shiver when his cell trilled to life.

"Hullo?"

"Mike? It's Jerry. Is this a bad time?"

Mike swallowed hard, nearly choking. He wiped his mouth with the back of his hand, Chris instantly forgotten. "Mmm. Hey. Hey, Jerry. Sorry. No, now's a good time. What's up? Any news?"

He gritted his teeth. He'd only met Jerry Foster once, but he could picture him easily. He was a large man, with a high voice, a decent suit, styled brown hair and half fat, half muscle, build. Mike had disliked the man the moment he'd walked into the loan office, hating the fact that his family's future rested on the diligence of a guy he trusted even less than he cared for him.

"I'm afraid I've got some bad news," Jerry said. He sounded like a little kid about to read from his report card. "The underwriters won't approve your application. They said the debt-to-income ratio is too high."

Mike squeezed 'til the phone creaked. "Last week you said it looked good."

"I did, but I also told you what you owe would play a factor."

"You said—"

"Mike, I'm sorry. But with yours and your wife's student loans, and her not working—"

"She's on FMLA. She still receives partial salary, and it'll only be another month or so before the baby is born..."

"I'm sorry, but according to the underwriters, even if your wife were still working full time the loan wouldn't be approved. Your debt to income is just too high. Now, if you were able to pay off some of that debt it would go a long way. I mean, you only have about nine thousand left on your Explorer. That could give the underwriters something to work with."

Jerry said it like a man who'd only believe what he'd said was true if someone else agreed with him first.

*If you've seen our finances, then you know how fucking impossible that is.* Mike pressed his fist against the brick of the building. Its grit pricked at his knuckles. "Well, uhm, that's going to be tough, Jerry."

"It's about the only way I can see this working."

Mike's stomach constricted as if someone was squeezing it with both hands. He punched the wall. "I'll see what we can do."

"Great! That's wonderful to hear. Oh, but don't forget to send us new bank statements before you resubmit, okay? The ones you gave us are about to expire."

"Can I fax them to you? I can print them from online and send them over."

He could practically hear Jerry shaking his head. "I'm afraid we need the originals. It's our policy whenever we're dealing with mortgages or personal loans."

Mike's breath whistled between clenched teeth. He glanced at his watch. SunTrust wasn't exactly around the corner and just getting to Jerry's office at Capital One would take twenty minutes anyway. He'd never get out of here before five. He couldn't even ask Patrick if he could leave early, not with Tom ready to dole out another ration of shit at a moment's notice.

"I've got a ton of work to get through tonight. I won't be able to get to you 'til Friday."

Jerry *tsked*. He actually *tsked* at him, as if Mike wasn't comprehending how important all of this was. "Well, just try to get it to me as soon as you can."

"Sure. You bet. I will. See ya, Jerry."

"Have a good day, Mike."

Mike hung up and just stood there trying to remember how to breathe without it hurting. That was it? That was the best Jerry could do after the reams of paperwork, the bank statements and mortgage documents, the myriad phone calls and the weeks spent waiting because the underwriters were dicking each other around? Just fucking...

His hand was wet. He didn't know why his brain thought this was important. It seemed a small thing to the rest of him, but his brain wouldn't let it go. Mike blamed the cold for the fact that he never felt it. The brick had scraped the skin off two of his knuckles, and a trickle of blood had seeped between.

It was a shitty distraction, but it kept him from dwelling on things he wasn't ready to think about yet. He walked back inside, jittery from the wind. Their office had a small kitchen, and it was there that he washed up. Alma gave him some Band-Aids but didn't ask any questions. The small nod of her head as she walked away was enough.

---

Tom's swagger ended the moment he closed the door. He leaned back against the wall and cursed quietly. It was only two flights of stairs from the parking lot to the main doors and a short hallway from his team's open-plan pit to his office, but still. He was out of breath and his undershirt clung to him uncomfortably. None of this was helped by the fact that his office had no right to call itself that, as far as he was concerned. Windowless and drab, the room was so narrow Tom could touch both walls at once with little effort.

It came with only the most basic essentials, and these were the sort of scarred and nondescript furniture every office in the last fifty years had seen. A desk, a small bookshelf, a two-drawer filing cabinet, and a chair. The chair wasn't even the office kind, leathered and wheeled. It was one of those straight-backed upholstered things they left out in the lobby for the customers, the ones that were supposed to be cushy in theory but were lumpy in practice. Even with a spare cushion he'd brought from home, Tom had to constantly shift just to keep his ass from going numb.

The only personalization he'd added to the place was the mini fridge plugged in by the door, and even this was more a necessity than a personal choice. He knew the others in the office didn't like him, and he didn't trust *any* of them not to fuck with his food while he wasn't around. So, into the mini fridge it went.

He punched at the keyboard and logged in to his computer. He'd just sat and started shifting this way, and that when his phone pinged. He fished it from his pocket.

*Balance Alert: This is to alert you that your checking account is overdrawn.*

"Fuck!"

Tom's foot lashed out at the filing cabinet, nearly toppling it. That invisible strap across his chest tightened as he jabbed at his phone.

*Thank you for calling The Bank of Oyster Bay. Your call will be answered in the order in which it was received. There is one person ahead of you at this time.*

Tom continued to curse as creatively as he knew how. There were more than two dozen emails staring at him from his inbox, several of them highlighted in an 'important' shade of red. But he couldn't deal with that now.

*Thank you for holding. Your call may be recorded for quality assurance.* "Thank you for calling The Bank of Oyster Bay. My name is Wendy. How may I help you today?"

"Yeah, I got an alert that my account was overdrawn."

Without pausing for breath, Tom spat out his account information in one long stream, one number bleeding into the next. A deliberate move. Tom had found that when it came to convincing people to give him what he wanted, it helped to knock them off balance first. He waited for Wendy to hesitantly ask him to repeat himself.

"Okay sir, just give me one second and. Yes. Okay, Mr. Downes, I've got your account open in front of me and it looks like an automatic payment for eighty-six dollars and fourteen cents came in this morning, but you only had fifty-four dollars in the account, so that's what put you over. I have here that the payment was to PSEG. Is that correct?

"Uhm." Tom coughed into his fist because it bought him a second to think. PSEG sounded like the electric bill. Or was it the water bill? Angrily, he shook his head. "Yeah. Uh, yeah that's right. Look, this is the third time you guys have done this to me."

"The bank didn't overdraw your account, Mr. Downes. That happened automatically."

"Don't try to tell me you don't make money every time it happens. What is it up to now? Thirty bucks a pop?"

"All banks charge overdraft fees, Mr. Downes. It's to protect the bank in case you write a check for more than you actually have."

"Yeah, the bank needs protection, while I end up thirty bucks in the hole."

"Actually, there was an additional fee for the returned payment. I'm sorry, but your balance is currently negative sixty dollars."

*"Are you fucking kidding me?"*

For the first time, Wendy hesitated. But when she came back, instead of flustered she sounded even more coldly professional.

"Mr. Downes, I will be happy to help you, but there is no call to use that kind of language."

"Happy to help me? Is that what you just said? Sorry, guess I just need a fucking minute to laugh that off."

"If you continue to use such language with me, Mr.—"

"Cause Wendy, I gotta tell you, of all the things I can't afford right now, that kind of language ain't even on the list."

"I am ending this call, Mr. Downes. Please makes plans to clear the balance at your earliest convenience. Goodbye."

"Wait, please!"

Tom shut his eyes and held his breath. He hated the way that came out. The desperation wasn't on the word 'please', but on the real list of things he couldn't afford. And among them, Wendy hanging up was definitely near the top. He waited but the click never came. So, for lack of better options, he just started talking.

"Look, I'm sorry. I didn't mean to jump down your throat. It's just, my wife and I are not in the best of spots, okay? I...We can't afford to keep dealing with all these fees. Please, I'm sorry. Can you help me out?"

The waiting game again. He listened to Wendy breathing on the other end of the line and tried to distract himself by imagining what she looked like, but nothing came. Finally, she sighed.

"According to your file, Mr. Downes, we waived the overdraft fee for you the last time this happened, so I can't do that again but…I can waive the taxes just this once."

"Thank you. Thank you, I really appreciate it."

"I can also transfer some of the money you have in savings over into checking. You have enough to clear the balance. And I can set a low balance alert on your account as well, just in case. You'll get a message on your phone if it drops below one hundred dollars."

"Thank you. Really, I mean that. How much have I got in savings right now?"

She told him and Tom had to dig his fingernails into his thigh to keep from cursing again. He tried to take a deep breath, but that strap was there, tight as ever. He squeezed out another thank you and, in a few minutes, Wendy had him back on the plus side. Tom had no idea how she managed it, but he thought she sounded cheerful when she said goodbye again.

He hung up and immediately failed at not thinking about his bills. There was enough to cover the mortgage on the first, but the rest were a question mark. There was something coming up in the next couple weeks, he was sure of it. Linda would know. And normally the money she brought in from the supermarket gave them a bit of breathing room. But that wasn't an option, not no more.

Deep in his head, a voice that sounded like it belonged to a guy who could still breathe whistled at him.

*Okay troop, if that's not an option, then what is? What can you do?*

Tom looked around his office and the hatred he'd felt walking in came roaring back. It wasn't just the fact that it was small, or that it would look exactly the same for whoever took over for him next. These were bad enough, but the crappy money was the real topper.

Six months ago, Patrick gave him the good news. New title, new office, new responsibilities. No power and the same pay. He was in charge of looking after half a dozen coworkers but didn't have an ounce of actual authority.

What could he do? Tom took hold of the anger in his head and draped it around his shoulders. It fit perfectly and why not? Anger and he went back a ways.

What could he do? He could damn well talk to Patrick about his money before the end of the day.

The Meeting

The conference room, like so many things in the building, wasn't designed to handle the large number of people currently occupying it. Seated at the eight-person table were a dozen coworkers, all wedged shoulder to shoulder, with purses, binders, and case notes scattered between them.

Arranged around their perimeter, like the outer ring of a tree, were another eight coworkers, each planted in gray plastic chairs designed in the days before the words 'lumbar support' were invented.

Mike, who'd arrived late due to a last-minute application, sat in the corner farthest from the door and leaned his head back against the wall. It was after ten in the morning, and he was already worn out. His arms sagged heavily at his sides, and his butt ached from the chair. When his phone buzzed with a text he didn't even move. For the moment, not moving was more important than being connected.

However, a few seconds later, his peace was interrupted as Alma plunked down across from him and smirked. She kept her phone low and sent a discreet text.

Mike fished out his phone and blinked wearily at it. The first message was from Claire, and it made him smile. She probably wanted him to pick up something from the store. He shook his head and decided to look at it later. He tapped on Alma's message instead and chortled.

*If I fall asleep right now, please don't wake me,* it read.

Mike typed away quickly, then hit SEND.

*No promises. If Patrick gives me the eye, I may have to kick you.*

Alma smiled and shook her head. *U R a true friend...I mean bastard.*

She put her phone away and, at the head of the table, Patrick stood up waving his arms.

"Okay, everybody. Let's get started."

There was no force behind it at all. Conversations continued as if he hadn't spoken. At Patrick's left, Tom disdainfully rolled his eyes.

Patrick must have seen the look because he grimaced and stood up straighter. He cleared his throat sharply and clapped his hands. "Okay! Okaaaaay! Come on guys. We're starting."

The conversations continued for another few seconds but eventually quieted. Everyone looked at Patrick. Half a smile grew on his face once he had their full attention. It withered away the moment he glanced at Tom, who glared back.

Patrick picked up his coffee mug, took a healthy sip, and held it at his side by his fingertips. "All right. I'm glad everybody could make it. I just have a few things to go over, so it shouldn't take up too much time. First—"

The door burst open behind him. He squeaked and jumped, sloshing coffee onto his shoes as Lauren tromped in.

"Sorry I'm late. Traffic."

She weaved her way through her coworkers and Mike cursed under his breath. There was only one empty chair left— next to him.

Patrick wiped up the mess with a handful of napkins. His voice was painfully high. "It's okay, Lauren. We just started."

Tom grumbled something Mike couldn't make out.

Lauren giggled. She hopped, tripped, and squeezed her way to the back of the room, smiling blankly at no one. In the corner, she turned around and fell backwards into the chair, slamming it against the wall with a sharp bang. "Sorry," she said, giggling again.

Mike studied her sideways and shook his head. Lauren should have been a very attractive woman. Straight black hair coupled with true mahogany skin. Her legs were long and slender, her waist slim, and on good days he'd seen her break out a smile so genuine it instilled a rash of smiles throughout the office.

But this wasn't one of her good days.

She was dressed paradoxically, rocking stylish leather boots while bundled up in a large black jacket that had gone to thread in some places. One pocket was torn, and stuffing showed through at the elbows and collar. She wore two pairs of sunglasses, one right on top the other. The outer set was huge and blocky like those reserved for cataract patients. The inner pair was leopard print and studded with rhinestones.

When she pulled these off, Mike had to fight not to wince. Her eyes were...well, dirty was a good way to put it. They were slow and dull, and the whites weren't really whites, more the yellow of old paper. She caught him looking and turned that vapid smile on him. Mike ground his teeth at the thought of a strained conversation.

"Hey Lauren," Alma said, saving him. "It's nice to see you. We missed you."

"Yeah, it's good to be here today. My back has been really acting up lately."

"So sorry to hear that. How's Joseph? Is he enjoying school now?"

Lauren's face bunched up, her top lip all but touching her nose in a curdled sneer. "Nope. He still cries every morning. I try to tell him, 'You'll make friends at school. It'll be fun.' But all I get is..." Her voice became nasal and shrill. "*No, no, no! I don't want to go! Please don't make me go, mommy!* Ugh. I love him, but he drives me nuts. He made me late this morning because he took so damn long getting dressed."

Alma leaned in and grinned like a hunting dog. "Really? I thought you said you were late because of traffic."

Lauren's mouth closed with a click, and she craned her neck to the side. Seconds passed.

"That too," she said finally.

Alma shot Mike a look, then sat back with a chuckle.

"Um, everybody? Can we please get back to the meeting now? Okay?" Heads nodded around the table and Patrick seemed to visibly calm. "Right. Good. Now, as I was saying, I've been informed that all the furniture has been moved into the new office. I haven't seen it yet myself, but Christine tells me everything looks great. Nice and bright and cheery with bigger offices and conference rooms. Which means…No more closets! Isn't that exciting?"

The lack of smiles was disconcerting, almost hostile.

"Um. Right, anyway. On to more serious things. The director has informed me that he needs us to prepare a spreadsheet of all our pending files and applications. Everybody you've worked with who still owes us paperwork. He needs it by Thursday so he can pass it on to the Regional Office before the weekend. Which means, I'm going to need all of you to go through your files and pass the information to Mike, so he can—"

"Whoa, whoa, whoa!" Tom's complexion had gone from ruddy to pissed off in two seconds flat. "What is this? Why does Mike get tapped for this?"

"Mike is coordinating the new applications already and this would just be—"

"Yeah, and if *you'll* recall, Pat, *I* brought up the suggestion that we make a spreadsheet two months ago." Tom swiveled from side to side in his chair. The constant squeak of the casters was like being jabbed in the ear with a paperclip.

"I'm uh." Patrick looked from person to person, searching for help. No one offered. "I don't remember you saying that, Tom."

"Yes, you do!" Tom slammed a palm against the table hard enough to snap Lauren out of her stupor. "We were sitting in your office, going over the encounters report, and I said we had to do something about pending files. That they were getting out of control, and you said—"

"What's Tom yelling about?" Lauren asked sotto voce, rubbing at her eyes.

Mike did his best to keep a distance between them but if he leaned away any more, he'd fall out of his chair. Lauren's strawberry perfume was as thick and cloying as syrup. It emanated from her so powerfully Mike couldn't breathe without it saturating his lungs.

"Is somebody in trouble? That why he's pissed?"

Mike swallowed hard. Her breath smelled terrible. The stale, putrid funk of someone who hadn't brushed in days. Mike closed his eyes and rubbed his jaw. "I have no idea."

Lauren squinted at him, then Tom, then finally shrugged and slipped on her cataract goggles again. In less than a minute her head drooped, and her breathing deepened. At the other end of the room, Tom made the mistake of pausing long enough for Patrick to get a word in.

"Th-Thank you, Tom. You're right. I-It probably shouldn't have taken this long to set up a spreadsheet for this. But all we can do now is get it done as best we can. You have your own projects to take care of. Mike can handle this."

The two men turned to look at him as one. Patrick was pure hopefulness in a white shirt and tie. Tom resentfully cracked his knuckles.

Mike nodded to them both and immediately Patrick looked relieved. He ran a hand through his hair and smiled at everyone.

"Great. Now there's just a couple more things we need to go over. HR has informed me that our appraisal packets are due next week and..."

They didn't even thank him. That was what galled Mike the most. They didn't thank him for taking on more work, on top of everything else he was already doing. Patrick hadn't even asked if he was willing to take it on. Just assumed.

*Oh, sure Patrick, ole' Mike can handle it. He's just doing the work of three fucking people; he can handle a bit more. Don't worry, he won't break.*

Though his face remained stoic, Mike's grip on the table tightened 'til the edge dug into his palms. Patrick kept happily talking about business appraisals, while Tom shot dark looks in Mike's direction.

Their 'short' meeting went on for another forty-five minutes before Patrick finally petered out. "Well, that's it. I don't have anything else to talk about. Does anyone have anything they'd like to go over?"

Heads shook emphatically.

"Great. So, let's get back to work. We've got a full day ahead, so I trust everybody to—"

For the second time that day, the door burst open. Only this time the woman who came through didn't giggle and didn't apologize. Sarah walked in with a look on her face that raised the hairs on Mike's neck. Her face was red, her fists clenched. She looked near tears and near to murdering someone at the same time.

Patrick obliviously sipped his coffee. "Oh hey, Sarah. You just missed the meeting."

Tom rolled his eyes even harder. "You've got great timing. Need to teach me that trick. Maybe I can use it to get out of next month's meeting."

Tom smiled at his own joke and a handful of others joined him. But Sarah only had eyes for Patrick.

"I'd like to talk about the new offices."

Her voice didn't shake an ounce. It made Mike straighten

up in his chair and it broke through Patrick's inattention like a hammer.

"Well, um. Sure, Sarah. I mean we already went over that. In the meeting. But if you want, we can talk about it in my office."

"No. I want to talk about it here. With everyone."

"I understand. But again, you missed the meeting. And we all have work to get back to."

"How many offices, Patrick?"

"Huh?"

"How many offices are there at the new location? Are there enough for all of us?"

Patrick's mug stopped right over his heart. The room went quiet, and Mike tasted something sour and panicky at the back of his throat.

"N-Now Sarah..." Patrick went pale and sweat marbled his forehead. "You know that management is doing all it can to make this transition as smooth as possible."

"No, we don't know that. How many of us are going to move to the new offices? Cause I know it's not all of us."

"That's ridiculous. Of course we're...Where did you?"

"My friend Lorraine, in HR. I saw her on my way to this meeting. The poor woman was in *tears*. She was cleaning out her desk, Patrick!"

"I'm sorry to hear that. But that doesn't mean we—"

Mike looked back and forth between them: the man of inexhaustible platitudes versus the woman who would not be placated.

"She said three other people lost their jobs the same day. She said this is only the start. How long have you known, Patrick?!"

She was close to screaming now. Or maybe that was just how Mike heard it. He couldn't be sure with the pounding in his ears. The hot coals of Sarah's insistence started to smoke and in a few seconds the room was on fire.

"My daughter starts high school in the fall."

"Jesus Christ, are you fucking kidding me?"

"Are we being fired?"

"...trying to buy a house."

"It's not fair for them to string us along."

"How long?"

"My husband just bought a new car."

"Janie's due in four months."

"How long do we have?"

It was Mike's most basic instinct for self-preservation that saved him. Patrick was a schmuck, but management liked him. Mike held off from adding to the baying crowd, keeping his mouth shut. People would think he was in shock. Even if they didn't, nobody would hold a grudge against him later for not joining in.

Patrick's face looked like it was about to melt off his skull. He waved his arms, sending coffee spattering across the table.

"All right, all right enough! Look um...hhhh, okay. I want you to understand this isn't official. The director still has to square away details with the contractors and there's a lot of, of...of you know. Details that—"

"For the love of Christ!"

"We deserve to know!"

"We have families! Lives to look after."

"How long do we have, Patrick?" Sarah thundered, her voice cutting right through the mass of noise.

"Two weeks." He wouldn't look at any of them. His eyes were on the dregs of his coffee.

Mike's stomach dropped. His arms trembled and there was a rock in his chest. No one said a word. The looks on their faces were divided between hatred and deep-seated worry. Glances were thrown in every direction, unspoken questions and shaken heads.

Mike turned just in time to lock eyes with Alma. *What the fuck?* she mouthed, lips trembling, skin pale. Even Tom, who usually had a comment about everything, was shocked into silence. Tremors shook him and his fingers scrabbled at the table as if searching for purchase.

Mike was nearly knocked out of his seat when Lauren propelled herself up and made for the door. She was heedless of any chair or person in her way, clipping shins 'til she blasted by Patrick with her phone to her ear.

"I have to...sorry. I have to call my...I'll be right back."

She slipped out the door and the frantic clomp-clomp of her heels echoed all the way down the hall.

"How long?"

Mike jerked, his head swiveling, and he wasn't alone. Alma was staring openmouthed at...

"You never answered about...Patrick? How long have you known?"

He'd never seen Margaret look so calm before. She sat neatly in her chair; hands clasped on the table before her. And though she stared at nothing in particular, Mike couldn't shake the feeling that if Patrick shifted even a hair, Margaret would have very primly eaten him.

Patrick blinked and shook his head. "Um. How long wh-I just said that, well..."

"No, you didn't. I want to know how long you've known some of us will be losing our jobs."

The room went quiet, the only sound the faint squeak of shoes on the floor. There was so much animosity in the room Mike could taste it on the back of his tongue. A mean, nasty flavor.

Patrick shifted his weight and started to cross his arms. A

defensive, 'I'm the boss,' stance. But, free from pressure, his left leg bounced spastically. He looked like he'd rather chew his own dick off than open his mouth.

"Margaret. Sarah...Everybody, look. I don't want any of you to think that I've been privy to any kind of special information. I am in the same boat as all of—"

He made to sweep his arm out and if it had been anyone else, Mike would have bet what happened next was intentional. But Patrick wasn't the kind. Not smart enough to be that much of an asshole. Patrick's coffee cup had been slipping by millimeters for almost an hour and the break from inertia with that final sweep was too much. It pulled the mug out of orbit and sent it flying across the conference table. It bounced, spattering several people in its wake, before tumbling end over end off the edge.

The sound of it shattering was almost as loud as the yelps, groans and curses as people stomped to their feet.

Patrick apologized profusely and was gone before anyone could catch him. His voice trailed down the hall, yelling something about paper towels. With their focus gone, everyone lost hold of the one thing that was keeping them together. They broke apart into small groups, all talking all at once.

"Do you think Lauren will come back?"

"And he sat on that for who knows how long?"

"Motherfuckers! Were they gonna wait 'til we were packing up and say, 'Oh yeah, you know what? You guys over here, don't even bother?"

"Who do you think Lauren ran out to call?"

"Her lawyer," three different people said at once.

Mike avoided looking at anyone. He didn't want them to see how much his eyes were burning. Or how his muscles were clenched like a doubled-up fist. He could taste bile at the back of his throat, and he couldn't even stand up straight. Forced to shuffle back to his desk, stooped like an old man, he swallowed hard, then again, because the things in his throat were too big, too sharp to get down on the first try. He stared at his monitor and tried to breathe without wheezing.

Heavy thoughts like loose bricks teetered on the edge of his mind. The mortgage and taxes, the car insurance, and the grocery bills, their student loans, and all the bills still to come. Things like diapers and formula and new clothes and vaccinations.

The stones fell and kept coming.

The water heater which should have been replaced a decade before they moved in. That tiny leak in the roof he noticed two weeks ago. The money everyone needs for when shit breaks at the wrong goddamn time.

Mike dug his thumbs into his eyes. He waited for the final thought to come rolling over the edge while desperately, fervently praying. *Please, please, please. Lord help me. I can't do this. I'm too tired. I don't have it in me. Please.*

So many hot, shameful tears had pooled in the corners of his eyes that when his cell blared, he thought about just letting it ring. Or pitching it at the nearest wall. But the tinny, grating little calliope kept playing and worked a kind of magic on him. It tapped into an ingrained habit and had his hand digging into his pocket before his brain could decide otherwise.

The display showed Claire's picture sandwiched between a red End and a green Answer. All that dark hair smiling at him, and he couldn't talk to her then, but he couldn't not answer it either. The calliope played and habit won out again.

He wiped his eyes and tapped green.

Claire picked up the phone and dialed for no other reason than because she wanted to hear his voice. It was just after eleven and if she knew Mike at all, he probably had a mouthful of chips at the moment, his ritual snack to see him through 'til lunch.

"Hey, babe...How-How are you?"

He sounded wrong. Bad wrong. "What's the matter? Is everything okay?"

"Yeah, yeah." He coughed thickly. "Just swamped. You caught me in the middle of uh..."

Claire bit her lip and tried to ignore the chill that had swept across the back of her neck. "Are you sure? I can call back. I just—"

"No, no! It's okay. I don't want to rush you off. I'm glad to hear from you. Is uh...Is there anything you need?"

Frowning, wishing she could see his face, Claire shook her head.

"No, I was just saying hi. Wanted to see how your day is going."

"It's fine," he said, too quickly. "It's been fine actually. Just crazy busy." He sounded genuinely surprised.

Worry embedded itself into her bones like a nail. "Well, that's good to hear. Nothing wrong with 'actually fine,' I guess."

"Yeah, right."

They both paused and Claire found herself searching desperately for something to talk about. A point or a fact that would serve to break up the awkwardness between them. She came up with nothing but thankfully Mike saved her.

"So, what have the two of you been up to?"

"Oh, nothing much. Just watching TV."

"Anything good?"

On the screen, a group of forty-something women sat around a table and screamed at one another. They all were of a type. Expensive jewelry and coiffed hair, designer dresses cut for maximum cleavage exposure. They each wore heavy makeup that did little to disguise the work they'd had done. One woman, the tallest and loudest of the bunch, was difficult to look at. Her lips were enormous, her nose far too small and her cheekbones absurd. For all the world, it looked like her face had come under new management—one which had built a whole new storefront underneath the old façade.

Guiltily, Claire shook her head. "Nothing good I'm afraid."

"Oh Lord. I know what that means." Mike chuckled, and the sound was like a pickaxe chipping away at her anxiety. "Which one are you watching?"

"Beverly Hills. Don't judge me."

"Oh, I'm judging. I am judging the hell out of you."

"Shut up," Claire said, finally able to laugh.

"How can you watch that crap? You always talk smack about people who watch reality TV."

"I *know*. But I'm home all day with nothing to do and there's only so much Food Network I can take."

"Okay, I'll give you that. But come on! There's got to be something else."

"Like what?"

"Well, didn't you always tell me you wanted to catch up on all the Seinfeld you missed while you were studying in college? That's eight whole seasons of nothing to keep you busy."

Claire summoned up as much horror as she could muster. "Days of forced isolation with nobody but Ina Garten and George Castanza to keep me company? I'd go kookyputz!"

The pause on the end of the line was even more pregnant than she was. Then, like startled birds, Mike's laugh flew into Claire's ear. "'*Kookyputz?*' Are you kidding me?"

"What? You've never heard that one before?"

"Do I sound like a man who's heard it before?"

Claire laughed along with him. Even Gabriel kicked

playfully at the two of them and their nuttiness. "Well. A wife should keep her husband on his toes. It's in the rulebook."

"Any more on my toes and I'll fall over," Mike hiccupped. "Love you."

"Love you too." Claire ran a hand over her belly until Gabriel quieted.

"Is there anything you need? Anything you want me to pick up on my way home later?"

Claire looked up at the ceiling for a moment and thought about it. "You know what, yeah. Now that I think about it. If you could grab some milk that would be great."

"Sure, no problem."

"*And curly fries!*" she added quickly, her stomach taking over in a fiendish coup d'état.

Mike cackled. "Curly fries, huh?"

Claire's tongue danced behind her teeth. "Babe, you have no idea. Crispy and salty, maybe with some cheese melted on top. God, I could just...*nom nom nom nom nom.*"

"I'll see what I can do."

"Will you really?"

"If you want me to."

She could tell he meant it and she loved him for it. Over the years Claire had come to believe that everybody needed someone who was willing to put up with their craziness from time to time. Smiling warmly, she shook her head. "You know what? You better not. I'm big enough as it is."

"Oh please, no you're not."

"You mean, I'm *not* big enough as it is? You want me to get bigger?"

"Will you...*Arrgh.* God help me."

Claire laughed so hard she hiccupped. "Y-You're the best! You know that?"

"Why? For the curly fries or for putting up with you?"

Claire grinned savagely. "Both. But I'm going to make you pay for that when I'm less in the family way."

"Something tells me I'll be looking forward to it," he laughed. "Listen babe, I'm sorry but I've got to get back to work. Thanks so much for calling. Hearing your voice was just what I needed."

"Happy to help. It was nice talking to you too. Try to stay warm, okay? I'll see you when you get home."

"Will do. Keep warm yourself. See you tonight. Love you."

"Love you too."

Claire hung up, still smiling. Within her, a small foot kicked once more. She drummed her fingers over her belly button. "Sorry, kiddo. No fries for us tonight." She made to pick up the remote again, then stopped. She looked left, right, then tucked her head down and whispered. "But keep hope alive."

Another little kick followed, and Claire laughed. She turned her attention back to the screen, quietly dreaming of her son dreaming of food.

———

Mike let out a long sigh and leaned as far back as his spine would allow. He concentrated on the little cracks and pops as his bones loosened up. He probably had only another minute before the others slumped in, the burden of their problems adding to the weight of his own. But he was grateful for the peace, however long it lasted.

Claire's call hadn't cured him of anything, but it broke up the pain in his stomach like a jack hammer through old concrete. All that heavy brickwork that nearly buried him was still there but sprinkled throughout were other things. Memories. Old ones. Including one in particular: dusty and too long unused.

He'd been in the area, running errands on a day now years past. He'd decided to stop in and see how his folks were doing. This was back when mom was merely sick, and no one was using words like 'final arrangements' or 'keeping her comfortable.'

He'd pulled up, windows down, Linkin Park blaring out like a frenetic horn. The smell of dried leaves was all around him. The garage door was open, and Dad was hunkered down, rummaging through old boxes. There were garbage bags and pails on every side and when Mike came up the drive, Dad smiled wide enough for the laugh lines to dig furrows along his face.

"Great timing," he said, pulling Mike into a hug. "Come and give your old man a hand."

Together they spent two hours cleaning out twenty years' worth of unwanted Christmas presents, broken rakes and snow shovels and furniture too beaten up to be worth a damn to anyone. All of it went to the curb and while Dad made a call to Special Collections, Mike grabbed a couple of beers out of the fridge.

From under the shade of their old porch, the neighborhood looked like it had been spun from a TV sitcom. Trim lawns, wide sidewalks, sprinklers and open bay windows letting in the breeze. It should have been idyllic. But it wasn't, and as he sipped his beer, Mike tried not to notice the way his dad sweated. Or how quiet the house was behind them.

The sweet and bitter hop of the beer masked some of it, but the sharp tang of Dad's sweat came through anyway. Dad's skin had a gray tint to it, packed in most around his eyes. It was a strange contrast for the years of pale sawdust he'd absorbed through years of building furniture. He looked too damn tired, even for a man his age.

Over his shoulder, the house should have had a rhythm to it.

Radio on, Mom singing, her black-silver hair swaying as she washed dishes or clipped coupons. By rights, she should have been out here with them, beer in hand with her cheek resting on dad's shoulder.

"So," Mike finally asked. "How is she?"

Dad took a long swallow. "She's okay. Just sleeping now."

Mike waited. More would come but only at his dad's pace. Minutes passed. The cold beer and the cool wind made the hairs on his arms stand up.

Finally, Dad looked at him. "She'll be all right, Mikey. She never let it beat her before. And she won't let it now." He huffed. "She's too stubborn for it."

That helped Mike smile a little. But the quiet wouldn't let him go. "How are you doing, Dad?"

The old man waved a hand and shook his head as if it was a silly thing to ask. "Oh, I'm fine son. Just fine. Don't worry about me."

Mike could see drops of condensation on the tips of Dad's fingers. Fingers that shook a little.

The question swung out like a broken branch. "What if…"

Dad's knuckles rapped gently against Mike's knee. He set his beer down between his feet and put an arm across Mike's shoulders. His voice had that bit of Brooklyn in it he'd never really left behind.

"Did I ever tell you about the time the Blue Bomb broke down?"

The Blue Bomb had been their name for Dad's old Buick. Big, ugly, and blue as the bluest Skittle. The thing was so beaten up that when Mike rode in the back, he couldn't put his feet down because the floor had rotted away. Every time Dad changed lanes, he could see the white divider strips fly by. But despite everything, the Blue Bomb never let them down. Trips to the city, the beach, work, school, emergency rooms. It took them everywhere they wanted to go.

Until the one night it didn't.

"To be honest, all I remember is one night you drove off, but somebody else brought you home."

Dad smiled and leaned back in his chair. "I was driving out to meet a client. The guy lived all the way out in farm country, right out at the end of the L.I.E. So I drove for over an hour, got to Exit 68 or 69 when all of a sudden, whoooosh." He threw up his hands. "It was shuddering, it was jerking, smoke coming out from under the hood. I pull over onto the shoulder and Blue just goes ka-thud. Doesn't even make a sound when I turn the key.

"It's late, it's farm country and it's three miles to the next exit. I hop out of the car and there's no one. It is as black and quiet as the end of the world. I'm standing out there in the dark with my little red gas can, feeling like I've got a sign on my forehead that reads 'Victim. Come and get me.'"

There was enough of his dad's old fear left to infect Mike and the skin across his back tightened. Being out there, you were as vulnerable as a man could get. Dad raised his hand and pointed, his voice weighted down by hope, incredulity and memory.

"The only thing I can see is the porch light of a small church I passed back down the road. So, I start heading for it. And in all my life, I'd never been so scared of my own footsteps. But that night...fields to either side of me, grass taller than I was." He shook his head and shuddered. "The closer I got to the church, the more it looked closed up for the night. No other lights, no cars I could see. I was just at the edge of the property when I heard it." He jerked a thumb back over his shoulder. "Tires. Coming my way." He shifted in his seat. "I turn and I see these headlights coming at me and I get a good grip on the gas can cause I'm sure whoever it is, I'm about to never be heard from again."

Dad paused.

"Car pulls up across the lane and stops. Window rolls down and this guy, about the same age that I am now, sticks his head out. 'Scuse me!' he says. 'That your car up the road?' I nod and he holds something out to me. I'm so scared I almost pitched the gas can at his head. But then I take a close look and..." Dad started laughing, big wracking guffaws that brought tears to his eyes. "It...It was his badge!"

Mike's own laugh flew out of his mouth like a catapult. Dad put his arm around him again.

"The guy was a cop! Said he'd seen my car broken down by the exit and decided to come looking for me." He wiped his eyes. "I was so happy to see him, Lord, I'd have kissed him! I started laughing even then. The guy probably thought I was a nut, standing there laughing on the side of the road. But he picked me up anyway and drove me to the gas station. He was even kind enough not to rub it in when he told me I'd been walking the wrong way!"

That did for both Mike and his dad. The tension cracked. Both men leaned back as their laughter echoed down the block. It went on and on, over the precision lawns and blooming flower beds, 'til it finally came to rest at the foot of the porch. Father and son picked up their beers and sipped, their eyes wet, jaws aching. Dad rolled the nearly empty bottle between his palms and talked to the blacktop.

"That wasn't the only bad night I've had, but life is like that sometimes. Big, black and scary for what feels like forever and then..." He rapped Mike's knee and smiled. "Take today I mean. If you hadn't shown up when you did, I'd have been out here 'til dark. I tell ya, one of us is getting old and I'm hoping it's you."

He plucked Mike's beer out of his hands and drained the

last swallow. Set the two fallen soldiers down next to each other with a clink.

"So, don't worry about me. And don't worry about your mom either. We've been looking after each other for longer than you've been around. That's just how it goes. When one is down, the other carries the weight. And as bad as things may look..."

Mike picked up the thread and smiled. "I get it. Thanks, Dad."

The memory ended as it always did, trailing away with a final picture of Dad's smile and how he tipped his head back to take in that impossibly blue sky.

Mike came back to himself, still at his desk, and a shadow made him look up. If he hadn't known better, he would've said Alma looked sick as hell. Not nauseous but heartsick. The gray cast to her skin, the droop of her lips, the slow way she moved. She looked besieged by a protracted illness. One with its hooks in deep.

"Fuckers. Goddamn pieces of shit," she said without any real energy.

Out of her purse she withdrew a creased and scruffy pack of cigarettes. He craned his neck to say something, but Alma was already on her way, purse on her shoulder, phone in hand and cigarette in the corner of her mouth. Mike was only mildly surprised to find it didn't matter. He had no idea what he would have said to her anyway.

On his computer screen a new email dropped into his inbox. He clicked on it out of pure habit.

Mike,

    Be sure to have everyone follow up with you regarding the Exceptions Report. Remember. Due by Thursday.

    Patrick

Mike rubbed furiously at the bridge of his nose. He tried to remember a time when his heartbeat didn't sound so damn off, or a day when he could take a full breath without wondering where the next hit would come from. That seemed only fair to him.

His dad's weary smile came to him again. Taken against the whole, it wasn't much. Mom's cancer came down like a crippling blow and things were hard, even brutal at the end, and now Mike was facing down potential unemployment and destitution with a baby just weeks away from seeing the world for the first time. But...

Mike looked at the papers in front of him. He snatched up the most immediate and set to. When that was done, he moved onto the next and the next and the next. Towards the end of his shift, he'd put a serious dent in the pile, bitten a chunk out of the Exceptions Report, and left a message for his buddy Chris about a potential job opening they'd talked about not that long ago.

Again, it wasn't much. But it was enough to prop up his spirits and keep him moving, which was all he really needed anyway. To not think for a little while 'til he got a better handle on everything.

He knew eventually he'd have to find a way to tell Claire the truth. The lie he'd given her was already curdling, and soon enough it would turn moldy and black. But not right then. He couldn't. His mouth and his brain were shut up tight, tumblers spun, pins locked firmly in place. He couldn't think about anything except that the sun was out. He gazed at it through the window, watched it turn the clouds red, pink and gold. Beneath it all, the wind stirred the trees, whipping the bare branches about sharply. Mike imagined that the air would smell of wood smoke and snow and for the first time that day, he didn't dread the thought of going outside.

Tom walked out of the office more tired than he'd ever been. It was five minutes after closing and his head was full of nothing. They'd drained him of everything, and 'they' might have included every living man on earth.

At his driver's side door he stood, key in hand, watching everyone else. Normally this would've been stupid. He cared about his coworkers only so much as...well. If he were being honest, he didn't give a fuck about his coworkers. Sure, they impacted his day but then so did the lights on Sunrise Highway. He treated them much the same, keeping an eye on them right up until the very last second then locking his front door and continue to not give a fuck about them until the next morning. But today he watched.

The way they moved reminded him of basic training, though he was damned if he could have said why. It was something about the way they clustered together, close but not so close they got in each other's way. All talking without looking at one another and when they neared a particular car, the owner would break away furtively, shoulders hunched, head down, eyes flicking left and right as if they expected a sniper to pick them off from one of the lampposts.

A sharp-edged wind whipped up and buffeted Tom, scraping through his hair like fingernails. His scalp tightened and he shuddered as a chill worked its way up from his toes to the back of his neck. The smell of snow was thick on the air.

Over the roof of her little grey Elantra, Alma's eyes narrowed with concern. "Tom? You okay?"

It wasn't 'til she spoke that the frigid hot pain in his hands hit him. He'd forgotten to put on gloves. His fingers were numb.

"Yeah. Yeah, I'm fine. See you tomorrow."

He turned away and miracle of miracles, managed to slip

the key in the lock on the first try. Slamming the door, he turned the heater on full blast. He sat staring straight ahead, shaking so much he had to clench his jaw for fear of it chattering.

Alma's car rolled away a few seconds later. He thought he saw her eye him before speeding off, but he couldn't be sure.

He sat and waited while his neck tightened up like someone was twisting a wrench. Twisting his head left and right did nothing, neither did jerking quickly to one side or the other. It was a huge fucking knot, and Tom knew it would stay that way unless he found the right...

Five minutes later the parking lot had emptied, and the knot was still there. The shaking hadn't stopped and, come to think of it, the rest of him wasn't feeling too hot either.

*Why won't the fucking car warm up?*

He punched the nearest vent but that did shit. He still couldn't feel the heat. He punched it again, then did it one more time before moving on to the steering wheel. The thuds were loud in the confined space, but the pain felt spot on. It loosened up that knot and took him out of the bad place he'd been in. And when he imagined faces on that wheel, those of his coworkers, his boss, his wife, he could just about feel their flesh and bone beneath his knuckles.

The last two shots he saved for himself. Clean across the jaw. For letting the shakes get to him too much.

When he was done, he felt...well, he felt like shit to tell the truth, but better than he had been. Sweat dripped down his back and his mouth tasted like it was full of hot dust. He rolled down his window and the cold was like a washcloth against his face. He let it sweep over him while he dug out his phone. Jimmy picked up on the third ring.

"Hey, brother. What's going on?"

"You home?"

"Yeah, just got here. Why?"

"I need a fucking drink."

"That shitty of a day, huh?"

"Meet me at Corley's in twenty minutes."

Tom knew Jimmy was more lucky than smart, but he'd never known him to be anything but loyal. Out of everybody he'd ever met, including his wife, Jimmy was the only one he could call up like this, voice tight and brittle.

"Yeah, course. Be there in a minute."

"Thanks, brother." Tom hung up and fished out his pack. The taste of the red, the smoke billowing around him nearly brought that wet cough back again but he held on. A drink would make him feel better.

He put the car in gear, twisted the wheel sharply and somehow managed not to glance at the office again before pulling out of the lot. The smell of snow was still there, even through the smoke, but he paid it no mind. Alcohol was the priority now.

"You gonna to do something with that, or just play with it?"

Tom looked up. Jimmy's face was the color of canned tomatoes.

"The fuck you talking about?"

Jimmy reached out and *plink*, flicked a nail against Tom's glass. "Just wondering if you're gonna drink that any time soon, seeing as Marcie went to all the trouble of pouring it like ten minutes ago. You pussy."

Jimmy smirked. He was enjoying the hell out of this, and all Tom could do was to run a thumb around the lip of the glass and glance at the clock. It was after five and he'd been staring at a long scratch in the bar top for who knew how long.

"Maybe the two of us are just getting acquainted. You ever think of that?"

"It's a whiskey not a woman, you jackass! Ain't like you gotta get her warmed up. What more do you need to know?"

"How she takes her coffee in the morning?"

Jimmy laughed, and Tom joined him even though there was no real happiness in it. The moment he'd arrived he'd taken his seat at the bar like he was planning to camp out there, giving Marcie the high sign to make damn sure she knew to keep them coming. But the second he took that first sip, he knew everything was wrong. The taste wasn't there. Oh sure, nothing was really missing. The peat and spice and that faint shadowy taste of the woods, they were all present and accounted for. But the relaxing burn was gone. Instead, that first sip had nothing but sour to it and Tom knew instinctively if he had any more of it...

"Brother, you have the weirdest way of getting drunk." Jimmy pounded a fist against his arm. "Okay, if you're not going to get hammered, then tell me what happened. You didn't call me over here for my company."

Tom rolled the glass between his palms. "You uh...you had any openings at your company lately?"

Jimmy's stool squeaked as he turned to look at him. His eyebrows had almost reached the edge of his comb over.

"No shit?"

"No shit. Company's downsizing and I don't like my chances. Anything you can put me on to?"

"Damn. Sorry, brother. It's off-season. The only thing we got right now is field work. You know, shoveling driveways and shit. The pay is—"

"I don't care what it pays Jimmy, I can make do. What I need is insurance."

Jimmy shook his head. "All we have is part time and we only give insurance to full timers. And well..."

"What?"

"Well, it's tough work. You're outside in the snow and ice all day. That ain't what you need."

"What the fuck does that mean?"

Jimmy glanced at him. "The way you been coughing lately. You sound like one of your lungs is orchestrating a prison break. You really think you'll be up for it?"

Like magic, that wet itch appeared in Tom's chest again. He almost took a sip but instead coughed into his fist.

"You...You aren't out in the...the fields." He knew his sputtering was barely clear, but he was damned if he'd start hacking up a lung in front of everyone. "I don't need...*hrnnnngrh!* I don't need to be fucking out there. Just give me a cushy office job, I'll be fine."

A new shade of red appeared on Jimmy's face. He leaned back and closed his eyes, taking a long, slow sip of whiskey. When he finally started speaking again, his voice had a tight rein on it. "No."

"No? That's all you got for me? Fucking *no?*"

"Yeah, that's right."

"Why not?"

"Cause I couldn't even if I wanted to, alright?! Look I know what everybody says, okay? That I just moved into this job and all I do is order Mexicans around all day." Jimmy opened his eyes and the look in them was as hard as the bar top. "Well, I didn't. I spent every winter for ten years out there shoveling. And every goddamn summer I mowed other people's lawns and bullshitted with housewives about what color rose bushes would look good in their gardens. I only got my desk job *last year* and I'm sorry your office is treating you like shit. But if you think you can just—"

"I'm s-sorry!" Tom hacked and the back of his hand was wet with spittle by the time he got it under control again. "What do you want from me, okay? I'm...I'm just...Shit." Asshole Mike's face flashed briefly in his head. "Look, I've got some guy breathing down my neck for my job."

"So, what? There's always one."

"You don't get it; I know guys like him. He's the kinda prick management loves. Never fights, never says shit about anything, his whole life's just fucking rosy twenty-four seven. Hell, if they stuck him with a Taser and all it'd do is get him to work overtime. Brother...I *can't* lose my insurance."

"If you're so fucking worried about it, why don't you just go to the VA?"

It was Tom's turn to close his eyes. He rubbed the back of his neck and sucked in air through his nose. "No."

"Come on, don't be an asshole about it."

"No."

"You served your time, and you need a hand. Nothing wrong with that. It's what the government's for anyway. Christ, it's about the only thing they're good for these days."

Tom huffed. He'd suffered through this same argument too many times. Linda harangued him about it for years. Hell, they'd even given him shit about it at work. Sarah, Alma, even Patrick, that wishy-washy little fuck who wouldn't last a minute in front of a drill sergeant before shitting his pants.

"I'm not doing it."

"Why not?"

"Because..." He took another swallow. The sour bit was worse this time, but he was too far gone to care. "Do you remember a while back when I thought I had the flu?"

Jimmy nodded. "I remember having to listen to you shitting, throwing up, and praying for death. Thanks so much for that by the way. That was a great call to get just before dinner."

"You're welcome. Always happy to ruin a friend's appetite. Anyway, I'm on the phone with my doctor, telling him everything and he's giving me shit about seeing me on short notice. I got so pissed at him I said fuck it. I went down to the VA, you know, just in case."

"Good idea. So, what happened?"

"I get to the hospital and I'm standing there like an asshole, with my paperwork that took me two hours digging through my house to find. And guess who's in line in front of me?"

"Patton."

"Fuck you. A marine."

Jimmy feigned shock. "So, a marine was standing in line with you. They're all over the place. Who cares?"

"He wasn't *standing*, you fuck. He was in a wheelchair, and you know why? Cause he didn't have any fucking legs."

Jimmy rocked back on his stool, looking like he couldn't think of a thing to say. Tom took another sip, warming up to the sour taste. "I was a supply clerk back in the day, not a grunt. I never even saw combat—they stationed me at Wiesbaden in Germany. I hardly ever left the base and the only time I came under fire was 'cause of my own people."

"You took friendly fire?"

"Yeah, some private got a Dear John letter from his wife and lost his fucking mind, grabbed an M16, and started just spinning around in a circle, popping off rounds."

Jimmy nearly choked on his next sip. "You're kidding? How'd you stop him?"

"I didn't. One of the drill sergeants came charging out of the barracks with his rifle. Man was wearing nothing but his boxers and his boots. He stood there, took aim, and just..."

Tom mimed holding a stock tight to his shoulder. He jerked back and forth on his stool making little popping noises at the bottles behind the bar. Jimmy howled and pounded Tom's shoulder.

"Christ! Did he kill him?"

"Nah. Cut him off at the knees though. Kid ended up

rolling around in the dirt screaming like a little girl." Tom flung out his arms and squeezed his voice 'til it could shatter glass. '*I'm hit! Dammit I'm hit!*'"

"The fucking pussy! What did the sergeant do?"

"Nothing. He just looked at him and said, 'Good, you stupid sonofabitch. I'm glad I didn't kill ya!' Then he went back to bed."

The two of them shook with laughter. They boomed, and wheezed, and coughed, and drank, and boomed all over again.

"Now...now that is some funny shit, brother." Jimmy leaned both elbows on the bar and looked like he was just concentrating on breathing.

"That's my problem. All I got is funny shit." Tom took another sip and nodded slightly. Yeah, he and the sour might be good friends by the end of the night.

Jimmy nudged him. "That why you don't want sign up?"

"You could say that, yeah."

"That don't make sense."

Tom sighed. "Look, you remember that Marine?"

"Legless Joe, yeah. What about 'im?"

"He's why I don't wanna sign up. Cause I still have ten fingers and ten toes. I came home with everything still attached."

"Except your dick. I think you left that at Wiesbaden."

"Will you shut the fuck up for a minute? I'm trying to tell you I'm not signing up for shit just so the government can go and take it away from some poor grunt who deserves it!"

"Boys?" Marcie was suddenly there, bar towel in hand and a warning on her face. "I have to ask you to keep it down. If you don't, then I got to cut you off."

Tom gripped his glass so hard he thought it would shatter. His lower lip drew in, ready to fire off a good old-fashioned fuck you, but a hand on his arm stayed him. Jimmy shook his head, a warning in his eyes, and Tom knew without a doubt the bouncer was right behind him.

Closing his eyes, he twisted his head to the right and finally, *finally* the fucking thing cracked. The relief was so welcome his whole body sagged.

"Sorry Marcie. Won't happen again. We promise."

Jimmy gave his own mumbled apology and by the time Tom opened his eyes, the bouncer was gone. Marcie slinked away a few seconds later and then Tom let out a long, low sigh.

"Is this the part where you try to cop a feel, or are you gonna take that hand off my arm?"

Jimmy sniggered and removed the offending hand. "Look, buddy. I get why you don't want to do this. But this is the government we're talking about here. If they can afford to pay for all Congress' bullshit, then they got enough to cover you without shortchanging Lieutenant Dan."

Tom nodded along, his head full of snow and clattering gears. Without warning, he started to chuckle. "Why the fuck am I friends with you?"

Jimmy clapped him on the back and flashed a conciliatory smile. "Same reason I'm friends with you."

"That's the fucking truth."

They laughed quietly together, though it did nothing to change Tom's mind. He still thought he'd be an asshole if he took benefits away from some other troop.

*That's not the only reason,* whispered the part of him that never learned when to shut the fuck up.

Jimmy and he settled into the quiet, each ordering another round. They shot the shit and drank and laughed but goddammit that noisy little voice in his head was right. He didn't want to go to the government for a handout—but not just because it was wrong.

He didn't want to go because he never thought he'd need to.

Mike carried the world away with him as he ran, dragging it through the dust of his footprints. He ran faster than he ever had in his life, fast enough to crack the ground with each step. He created a roar that filled the Earth from end to end.

In his path, right at the edge of the horizon, stood a man, wild-eyed and grinning. He had his arms spread wide like he could stop Mike by insanity alone, and Mike couldn't be sure if he wanted to save the man or mow him down. He thought of slowing, of turning aside, but at the same time his limbs pumped faster, and his heart thundered, and his own cheeks hurt from grinning so wide the closer they came to one another. As momentum drove him on, Mike saw the way the man's fingers twitched and his muscles jerked, and he knew he was thinking of running too. He knew it as sure as he could taste the sunset just up ahead.

The man wanted to get the hell out, but he wouldn't. Not couldn't, but *wouldn't*. He was as trapped as Mike, and as they came within screaming distance the man screamed for both of them in rage and pain and horror, the sound rising 'til it drew iron nails down the back of Mike's skull, 'til it dug deep and burned away everything he had in unending incessant shrieking —*beepbeepbeepbeepbeepbeepbeepbeepbeepbeepbeepbeep-*

"Fuck!"

Mike pounded his fist on everything within reach. The alarm, the nightstand, the side of the bed. But the goddamn fucking beeping wouldn't stop. Blindly he yanked the iPod out of the docking port. Nothing.

Finally, he half fell, half rolled out of bed, his knee cracking against the dresser, and yanked the plug out of the wall. The silence that followed didn't even last ten seconds.

"Babe? You okay?"

Mike squeezed his eyes shut, pressed the heels of his palms against his temples. His knee throbbed painfully, and his back was twisted. Slowly, he righted himself. "I'm okay, babe."

What happened?" Claire's hair stuck out in crazy directions. She sat up and Mike saw the crust of dried spit in the corners of her mouth.

"The alarm clock. I don't know what's wrong with it, I'm sorry."

Atop the chest of drawers in the corner, the cable box blinked. It was five thirty in the morning. Half an hour before his alarm was *supposed* to wake him up.

Claire yawned and ran a hand through her hair. "Sorry, babe. You haven't had it that long, right?"

"A couple of months."

"Should still be under warranty, then. Take it back to the store, maybe they'll exchange it." Claire straightened out the covers and laid back down. "Come back to bed, it's still early."

He wanted to more than anything. Wanted to curl up and let the warmth of her put him back to sleep again, but he was too wide awake. Sadly, he shook his head.

"I'm going to jump in the shower. Maybe I'll make myself some breakfast before I head out."

Claire frowned and reached out a hand. "Really sorry, babe."

"It's okay. Try to get some sleep. I'll be fine."

He watched her roll over and then stretched as best he could. His knee hurt like a malicious chiropractor was wrenching on it, but he rubbed it 'til the pain subsided. By the time he was done, Claire's deep and even breathing had returned. He gave it another minute then gently reached out and brushed his fingers through her hair. He smiled as she mushed against his hand like a cat and seemed to sink even deeper into the bed.

Chuckling soundlessly, Mike kissed her shoulder then grabbed his robe and headed for the shower. Later, as he bundled up, an impulse directed him to the closet for a plastic bag.

Nothing woke Claire again, thankfully. Not the closet door's hinges nor the clatter of the alarm clock as he stuffed it in the bag. He kissed her cheek before he left. She smelled like the cotton sheets and sweat and a sweet smell that he acquainted with her being a mother. Sometimes he pulled her close just so he could get a lungful of it. Like vanilla when it was baking.

Wishing for the hundredth time he could crawl back in beside her, Mike trudged out the door.


Mike's office might have been on the second floor, but the cafeteria was in the basement at the back of the building, a design choice no one liked or understood as it took several precious minutes off a thirty-minute lunch.

He tucked his water bottle under one arm and tried to both dig through his briefcase and navigate the stairwell. He'd been meaning to plug Chris' work number into his cell for a while now but had never gotten around to it. Finally, after nearly tripping twice, he fished out his little reminder notebook and then grabbed his cell. The landing was empty, but he still kept one ear open for anyone coming down. He didn't want to run the risk of it getting back to management that he was making alternative arrangements.

The phone rang and Mike kept his shoulders square, his back straight. Chris picked up on the sixth ring.

"Chris Ward."

The difference between them was right there, in those

words. Not the two words Chris said, but in the ones unspoken. He never said who he worked for or asked 'how could he help you' because he never had to. By the time he finished saying his name, whoever was on the other end knew they'd found someone in charge.

"Hey, Chris. It's Mike. How's it going?"

"Mike! Hey, it's good to hear from you. How you been?"

"Good, good. How about you?"

"The same." He sounded like it.

Shortly before they both received their MBAs, Chris managed to score a hotly sought-after internship at a major pharmaceutical company. And while he liked Chris a lot, listening to his smooth well rested voice vibrating in his ear, Mike always got the impression that when they both said they were good, one of them was lying.

"Glad to hear it brother," Mike continued before the pause could get too long. "I just wanted to check in and see if you'd heard anything new about a job?"

"Nnngh. Sorry, buddy. I haven't heard anything. I've been talking you up to the boss for a month, but he says Fiscal is dragging its ass."

Mike brought his fist down hard against his thigh. "Why, what's wrong?"

"Ehhh, some bullshit about getting approval for funding. They won't open up the position officially until the money is in place first. The company has been cutting corners on so many things, nobody wants to move until the money is secured."

Mike poured some lightheartedness into his voice and threw up his hands. "Hey, if it's money they're worried about, I don't have a lot of needs. They could put me in a broom closet for all I care. I've been working out of one long enough, it's almost comfy now."

The pause he heard down the line was like the silence that

follows a bad comedian.

"Is it that bad over there, man?" Chris asked with real concern.

Mike took a deep breath and rubbed the bridge of his nose. "It's uh. It's getting there. Yeah."

Chris' sigh swept into his ear and suddenly he *really* wanted to get off the phone. Talking about this to anyone was tough but that sigh from Chris, a good friend, needled Mike. His face turned red, and his hands became slick.

"I'm real sorry to hear that, buddy. Wish there was something I could do. I'd talk to my boss again but with Fiscal dicking around, I'd get more accomplished if I pissed in my trash can."

Mike chuckled and even to him it sounded real. His stomach felt looser, the way a good sneeze could break up a cold for a few seconds. He smiled into the phone. "You should pitch that to Fiscal. Tell them it would save them on the water bill every month."

Chris laughed. "Yeah, it might. Don't think our cleaning crew would be too happy with me, though."

Mike's gut opened up a little more. "Maybe not."

The laughter went on for a few seconds, but Chris finally cut it off. "Seriously, man. If there's anything I can do..."

"I appreciate that. Thanks."

"If you need, you know. Something to see you through, I can—"

"*No.*" The word came out so fast it almost split Mike's lip. "No, no, no. We... we're good. I appreciate it. But...yeah, we're nowhere near there yet. We'll be okay."

Mike closed his eyes and listened to the silence on the line. His stomach hurt worse than ever and his heart beat fast, much too fast. He heard Chris draw in a breath.

"Are you sure? Because it's no problem, really."

Mike's jaw clenched. "Yes, uh yeah. Don't worry, we'll be okay. Just let me know if anything comes up about the uh..."

"Sure, you got it. No problem," Chris said, stilted. Uncomfortable. "How about we get together next week? Y'know, grab a beer together. I haven't seen you and Claire in—"

"Yeah, I know. It's been a while. I'm not sure though, let me check my schedule and I'll get back to you."

"Sounds like a plan," Chris said, a touch hopeful again. "Stay well, okay?"

"You bet. I'll talk to you soon." Mike hung up without waiting for a goodbye. He sat there for a moment, forehead pressed deep into his palms. His gorge threatened to rise but he swallowed hard until it subsided.

*Goddammit. Where the fuck do you get off?*

Mike ran a hand roughly through his hair and tried to fight off the anger. Chris was one of those rare friends who'd stuck around despite the pressure of years and distance and screw-ups. Close since high school, they'd seen each other through more tests, breakups, crappy teachers and worse jobs than Mike could handle remembering.

*So why do I hate him so much right now?*

Leaning against the wall Mike sucked in one long breath, hoping it would cool the overheated gears in his head, but when he looked down at his phone again, he scowled. There were only ten minutes left on his lunch.

---

Tom walked into the Stop & Shop with a hunger that beat at the back of his head like an insistent knocking, but it wasn't food he was really after. Having failed to bully Patrick into giving him a raise, and with that damn 'Low Balance Alert' *pinging* at him earlier in the day, that left getting piss drunk as his only option.

Through the sliding glass doors, a wave of heat blasted, the little walkway so hot it was oppressive for the few seconds it took him to cross it. Inside the main store though, a significant chill pervaded. He grumbled as he cut his way through the produce section like a getaway car was waiting for him outside.

At the deli counter he slowed just long enough to snag a rotisserie chicken then swerved, cartwheels squeaking. He rolled on to Kraft Mac & Cheese, bread, frozen pizzas and only when he had his hand wrapped around the cheap, thirty-ounce bottle of knock-off Coke did he pause.

Straight across the aisle was a cold case packed with what looked like half a block of beer. The usual suspects took up eighty percent of it but in the far corner sat the craft beers, chilling quietly. Chocolate stouts, lambics, ales fermented in the bottle. Tom picked one up.

Gold liquid under a gold label and an embedded cork. The name was written out in copperplate but still had too many consonants. If he tried, it would come out sounding like an axe hacking away at a tree. He ran a thumb across the label and was surprised when his face heated. A memory came to him, loud and stupid, like a drunk friend tripping into the wrong room.

Except this was a friend he really didn't want to talk to so, ducking his head, he slipped the bottle into his cart and then headed for the registers. Even this late on a weeknight, the lines with actual cashiers were long. At the self-check lane, he tapped the screen with his knuckles and already had his credit card out when an electronic voice pinged.

*Your order contains an age restricted item. Please wait for a customer service representative.*

Tom scowled and shook his head. It took a conscious effort not to roll his eyes as he watched a short, fat girl in a purple smock waddle over with her keycard.

She looked at the screen, then at him. "Can I see some I.D?"

Tom blinked, then burst out laughing. He clapped her playfully on the shoulder, still shaking his head. "Good one. You almost had me there." The look on the girl's face cut his smile off at the knees. A kind of creeping, stupefied shock worked its way up his spine. "Are you serious?"

"I'm afraid it's store policy, sir." She couldn't have sounded more bored or less apologetic if she tried.

Tom stared at her. Her cheeks were a mass of whitehead pimples, and her right ear was completely taken over by tiny black diamond earrings. He saw a little flash tattoo of a skull on the side of her neck that undulated when she swallowed. If she was even a quarter his age, he'd kiss the soles of her sneakers.

He coughed words at her. "You don't need to see my ID."

"I'm afraid I do, sir. I can't sell you alcohol without it."

"Come on, honey, this is stupid. I'm three times your age." He pointed at his gray hair. "This isn't a dye job."

"It's. Store. Policy. Sir."

Tom's jaw tightened and a familiar pressure filled his head. This was way beyond the last thing he needed. He'd been thinking about stopping at the liquor store after this for a fifth of Irish, but the beer had caught him off guard. He wasn't ready to deal with the memory yet, but he couldn't leave the bottle behind either.

With a quick glance at the screen, he fished out his wallet.

Beside him, the girl visibly relaxed back on to her heels. One corner of her mouth curled up and she held out a hand for his ID.

Tom slapped two tens and a five into her palm. He smiled as she blinked mutely up at him. He managed to squeeze past her and start bagging his groceries. She came back to life just as the beer vanished.

"Sir? Sir! You can't just leave with that. *Sir!*" Her shrill voice attracted attention. A guy in a purple T-shirt started to walk over. Tom stood up straight and looked at him hard. The guy, a balding man in his thirties with glasses and acne scars, stopped where he was. He was shorter than the girl and not even half as wide.

Tom kept his eyes on him as he finished bagging. The girl was losing her fucking mind, yelling at both of them now. Tom smiled at her and headed for the door, tossing a one finger salute over his shoulder. The girl's shrieks followed him into the sauna entryway but were blissfully cut off by the winter outside.

Still smiling, he walked across the lot and fished out his keys. Dropping the bags onto the passenger seat, he plopped behind the wheel with a satisfied sigh. But the key scraped over the steering column when he tried to put it in the ignition.

He tried again and smacked the lever for the windshield wipers, sending them squeaking across the dry glass. Again, and his fingers jammed against the steering column. It took him several seconds to accept that his hands were shaking.

The keys slipped out of his fingers and landed at his feet. He closed his eyes and gripped the wheel hard 'til his knuckles were white and the pain arced all the way up his forearms. He looked out the windshield at the trees swaying in the wind. The girl's face came back to him. Round, ugly and shit-kicker dumb.

The way she'd spoken to him. Automatically assuming he'd go along with her stupidity. And the manager. A lightweight fag in a purple blouse who Tom could tell was close to pissing himself as he neared.

But the thing which got to him most, that filled him with boiling piss and vinegar, was the pounding of his heart. Sweat broke out across his forehead and he had trouble getting his breathing under control. No matter how hard he tried, his brain wouldn't stop ticking.

*What will they do next time I come in?*

*There's nothing they can do.*

*I paid for what I took. They're not gonna do anything except smile and ask if I have any coupons!*

For a long minute he had a picture of a dozen eyes, customers' and clerks' alike, boring holes into him but eventually the piss and vinegar won out. His heartbeat slowed, and the sweat dried up on his forehead.

In control again, but more tired than he'd been in months, Tom cracked his knuckles. He ran his hand along the floor mat, then slowly inched the keys into the ignition.

A twist of his wrist and suddenly he felt better, more in control now that he had a living means to escape beneath him. He rolled down all four windows because fuck the cold, he could deal with it. Turning on the radio, he cranked up the volume as high as he could stand. The freezing wind swept through before he even pulled out of the parking space, but he didn't care. Home was just down the road, his favorite song was playing, and he *needed* to let everyone know he was there.

Tom twisted the wheel hard. Tires screeched as he drove out of the lot. Over the wind, he shouted along with the radio, his voice drummed up from his days in infantry. *Sound off, Motherfucker! Sound off like you got a pair!*

As he drove off, more than a few customers looked at one another, their faces perplexed. He grinned madly at them, putting his foot down 'til the engine roared. He chose not to register that many of them shook their heads and turned away as if what they saw was something pitiful.

---

Walmart wasn't crowded, at least not for Walmart, but Mike still had precious little good will left in the tank.

Between his conversation with Chris, a dozen walk-ins, two conference calls and a thirty-minute lecture from Pat on a 'very important' Performance Measure they weren't meeting, Mike was drained down to his reserves. In fact, he'd argued with himself about even coming here, but he couldn't do another morning of that goddamned beeping.

The alarm clock tapped against his leg as he waited in line, propelled by his body's inability to hold still. He swayed as he waited, sandwiched between an elderly black woman clutching a DVD player and a pasty-faced woman whose cart was so crammed with stuff it was almost as wide as she was.

Pasty-face stood before the clerk in designer jeans and a faded tank top, both stretched almost beyond capacity. Her arms waved as she talked and every time she leaned over the counter, the tank top rose, revealing rolls of flesh and a bright red thong. Mike kept having to turn his head away, wishing he could Purell his eyeballs.

"Listen, listen. I don't have *time* to argue with you. I've got my kids sitting in the car. I just want to return this stuff. *Why* is that so hard?"

The clerk was a short blonde college student with bright pink nails who looked like she desperately wanted to dig a moat between the woman and her. "Ma'am, you don't have a receipt. And that's at least eight hundred dollars' worth of stuff. You can't just return it."

"I *know* how much it is. They were all *gifts*. Now I want to return them."

"Ma'am, you don't have a receipt."

"Then give me store credit."

"I can't do that either ma'am."

"Why not?"

"Because I saw you when you walked in, and you didn't have all this stuff with you."

"Are you accusing me of *stealing*? You *saw* me? Out of all these people? You remember seeing me?"

"You're very memorable, ma'am."

The woman leaned even further over the counter, her voice rising, but Mike turned away again, glancing instead at the line of people behind him. He saw dirt caked jeans, sweatpants, unwashed heads, ratty sneakers and one woman wearing actual fuzzy slippers.

Mike twisted so far around that he caught the eye of the elderly woman with the DVD player. She stood out like a remnant from another time, one where people still remembered what personal grooming meant. Her gray hair was combed, her clothes simple but neat, and she stood with an easy, reserved calm.

Mike smiled at her then inclined his head, indicating everyone in the lines around them. She turned and looked quickly, her head shaking then shrugged and gave Mike a sad, knowing smile. In his buttoned-down shirt, tie, dress slacks and shoes, the two of them looked like they'd come for a town hall meeting but were the only ones who'd remembered to dress.

"I can help who's next!" a voice called out.

Mike turned to see a dark-haired kid, pudgy and pale, waving at him. He headed over.

"Hi." Mike said, putting the alarm clock on the counter then reaching into his pocket for the receipt.

"Hi, how can I help you?" The kid's voice was breathy and tired. His nametag read 'Brian.'

"Yes. I'd like to return this please."

Brian looked in the bag. "Do you have the box it came in?"

*Who the hell keeps the box?* Mike bit this back before it could leave his mouth. "No, I don't. But it doesn't work anymore, and I'd like to return it."

Brian eyeballed the receipt, one eyebrow significantly higher than the other. "It's more than ninety days old."

"I understand that, but it doesn't work. It stopped playing

music and yesterday it woke me at the wrong time."

"I understand, sir. But it's more than ninety days old. We only accept returns if it is less than ninety days since you bought it."

Mike rubbed his face with one hand. "Then I'd like to exch—"

"I'm sorry sir, but it's the same policy. No returns *or exchanges* after ninety days."

"Look..." Mike could feel a headache forming behind his left eye. "I didn't just walk in here, pick this up off the shelf and come straight here. I'm not trying to cheat you." He said it loud enough that the woman next to him gave him a look as ugly as holy hell. He ignored her and focused on Brian. "I'm just tired of getting woken up at the wrong time and to the wrong sounds. For the last three days, it's been nothing but a shrill beeping."

Brian shook his head. "I understand, sir. But you bought this more than ninety days ago."

"You keep saying that!" Mike put more into it than he'd meant to. On another day he probably would've apologized, but right then somebody was shoving a golf ball into the back of his skull. Mike massaged his temples and kept going. "I only bought this thing a couple of months ago. And it's already broken. Things shouldn't break down in a couple of—"

"More than *three* months, sir. Almost four. See? It says it right here on the—" Brian held up the receipt and pointed a pudgy finger, but Mike snatched it out of his hand.

"I can read! There's no reason to insult me." Not as loud but twice as harsh.

"I wasn't trying to insult you, sir. I'm sorry if that's how you took it." Brian's voice had a little something extra in it now. Was it fear?

"Just...Just exchange the machine."

Brian was staring at him. No—staring at his *eye*. "I still can't do that, sir. We can't change store policy."

The pressure in Mike's head was becoming unbearable. It beat against his eye faster than his heart was pounding. Any worse and it might propel it right out of his skull like a cannon.

*How about that, Brian? Would you change store policy if my eye suddenly shot out and hit you in the face?*

Mike covered his left eye with the heel of his hand and pressed in 'til it watered. "I'm not asking you to change store policy. I'm asking you to honor the fact that a product you sold me broke down in a couple of months."

"I'm sorry but if you have a problem with the product, may I suggest you take it up with the manufacturer?"

"And may I suggest you stop talking to me like I'm a f—"

His phone went off with the four-note trill of a text. "Excuse me," Mike said, instantly regretting it.

It was Claire: *Hey babe! Can u do me a favor? Pick up some more Tylenol along with the milk on your way home? I really think my hips are trying to do me in. Thanks!*

Already half blind, Mike struggled to see through those little white shadows, which were returning again. "I don't care what your policy is."

*You got it, Love,* he typed.

"It's not fair that something only a couple of months old..." he went on, fingers still flying.

*Be home s—*

The screen froze.

Mike tapped and tapped and tapped away but it was as unresponsive as his shoe. He lost his train of thought. "I um. It's just that. I shouldn't have to..." He punched the home key again and again, accomplishing nothing.

Brian butted in. "Sir. There really is nothing I can do for you. You need to speak to the manufacturer. Now, please step aside. There are other people who need—"

Mike kicked the counter so hard, every clerk on the line jumped. "I don't care what other people need! You're not done helping me, yet!"

Brian, wide-eyed and paler than ever, edged back to the desk again. "S-Sir," he said quietly. "I can't help you."

Mike held down the power button, silently counting in his head.

The screen was still frozen. Nothing he did was working and from somewhere close by, some asshole started to yell.

Mike swung without thinking. He raised the phone high and brought it down on the edge of the counter. His head pounded, he was going on full blind, someone wouldn't stop yelling and the impact of phone to counter went all the way up to his shoulder. The phone wasn't working, his job wasn't working, even the simplest things weren't...

"Sir? Sir, maybe I can help you?"

This voice was different. Calmer, older, more authoritative. Mike looked up and found a woman smiling at him from behind the counter. Late forties, light brown hair threaded with gray, the beginnings of crow's feet.

"We'd like to apologize for holding you up like this. I'm sure it's very frustrating for you. If you just give me a moment, I will go ahead and process your full refund. How does that sound?"

Mike hadn't seen her arrive, but she stood as if she'd thrown Brian bodily behind her. The rest of the store had gone quiet. No one in line was talking and even the ring of the nearby registers sounded muted. Mike's left eye looked out on a sea of white and his right was too blurry to read the woman's nametag.

"Thought...I thought I could only get—"

"We're going to make a special exception in your case, sir." She looked away from him only once, tossing a glance at the stock-still Brian. 'Go!' she mouthed before turning back, her smile as brittle as ice.

"Tha's fine," Mike mumbled. His head hung low, and his arm swung loose at his side.

It took her less than thirty seconds. The clock and receipt disappeared, and in their place came cash. He pocketed it without saying a word.

"Here you go, sir. Have a nice day," she said at last, and the worst part was that she hadn't even said it unkindly.

It wasn't 'til he walked away that he noticed a good eight feet of space had cleared around him. Even the large pasty woman, the thief, kept her distance. Two tall men, broad-shouldered and wearing yellow security vests, watched him go. Just before he reached the doors, Mike looked back to try and catch the old woman's eye again. Hoping to find some momentary camaraderie still remaining.

She'd moved up to the counter and was talking with the manager who'd taken over for Brian. Right as the front doors slid open and the biting wind blew in, she turned. But what Mike saw in her eyes only amplified the pressure in his head. It laid a heaviness about his shoulders that stayed with him the whole rest of the way home.

With one hand braced against the wall, Claire leaned into the shower and twisted the faucets. Icy cold and steaming hot water met in the bottom of the tub and mingled like two old friends. Using her fingertips, she tested the water 'til it was perfect, and then groaned aloud.

Growing up, Claire had never been a bath type of girl. From the time she was old enough to handle herself, she'd devoutly chosen the shower for its economical speed. "Baths are for babies and old people," she remembered saying to her mother. People with time on their hands.

But as she grew older and life got busier, she discovered two things.

One was that while a shower might get a girl out the door quickly, a bath could be like a personal haven. And though she loved Mike dearly, she secretly suspected he enjoyed this time apart at the end of the day. She took it as his silent acknowledgement of their shared need for space, even from each other. A similarity which, thankfully, had never rankled.

The second thing she discovered was that when she'd said those words to her mother, before she had worries like work and bills and a baby on the way, she didn't have the first clue how precious having time on her hands could be.

As she waited for the tub to fill, Claire used the time to undress and studiously avoid looking at the bathroom mirror. She knew from hard experience nothing good ever came of it.

She'd made the mistake once, about five months in, and she'd nearly recoiled at the sight. Her face was puffy, her skin blotchy, giving her cheeks a dough like consistency as if she'd been kneaded during the night by a baker half in the bag.

Though she'd cleaned up only the night before, her hair still felt lank and tangled and the rank smell of sweat clung to her. She knew the house might not have been much to some, but the bathroom suited Claire right down to her shoes. The previous owners had been an elderly couple, which explained the thick steel handgrips embedded into the walls.

As a newlywed on their first walkthrough, Claire had been overjoyed at the tub's deep, jet-festooned state. And as a woman heavily besieged in the family way, she thanked every deity she could think of for the simple joy of being able to lie fully in warm, scented water while little jets did their damnedest to massage away all her aches and pains.

Closing her eyes, Claire did her best to stretch, rolling her neck and shoulders and pushing out her hips as much as the weight of her son would allow. Half smirking, she drummed her fingers lightly over her belly button.

"No offense, kiddo. But the second you come out, Mommy is going to the chiropractor."

The crick in her lower back felt about the size of a toddler's fist. It and the pain wore her down and drained her of energy. By rights she should be fast asleep the moment her head came anywhere near a pillow. But with how often she had to pee during the night, and Gabriel's tiniest movement waking her instantly, sleep was difficult at best.

Most days, she ended up taking catnaps while embedded in what she'd come to think of as her beach head on the couch.

"Scratch that, my handsome boy. The first thing I'm going to do once you're out in the world is sleep for a month."

At last, the tub was full, and Claire settled into it with a long, satisfied sigh. She dipped back and dunked her head, let the water drip down her spine, felt the warmth soak into her by inches, and it wasn't until she reached for it that she realized she'd forgotten a washcloth.

"Shit." She looked down. "Pardon Mommy's language, kid." Claire craned her neck towards the door. "Babe? Baaaabe!"

A few seconds later a soft knock came. "Everything okay?"

"I forgot a washcloth, I'm sorry. Would you mind?"

The door opened and Mike swept in. He plucked one off the small stack in the cabinet by the door and held it out.

"Thank you," Claire said. "Sorry again."

"Don't worry about it. S'no problem."

Claire thought he'd head back out but instead he lingered. He'd been worryingly quiet from the moment he walked in the door. Chin jutting grimly, cheeks pale, eyes locked on an invisible problem.

Several times Claire had asked if he was all right, but her husband was as shut tight as a safe, his only answer a shrug and a mumbled 'sure.' If he'd expected that to allay her fears, it crapped out like a car held together with crazy glue. She'd spent the rest of the meal wondering what was going on in his head.

Right then though, as he leant over her, it was no trouble at all to guess what he was thinking.

He stared at her intensely, as though he were drinking in every detail. The tub, her hair, the swell of her belly, the gentle lap of water between her breasts. His lips were parted, and his cheeks were flushed.

Her own skin colored in the heat between them.

"Knock it off, you," she said, squirming slightly, feeling warmer than she'd been a few moments ago.

"What?" he asked.

"Don't give me what! You know exactly what you're doing."

He shrugged easily, smirking at her. "A guy can't look at his wife?"

"No. No he can't."

"I can't help it. You look good."

Claire rolled her eyes and snorted. "Yeah well, there's a lot more of me to see these days. I'm kinda hard to miss."

"Oh, would you stop? I mean it. You look really good."

Remembering her horrified glance in the mirror, Claire wanted to say he'd lost his mind, but...leaning against the cabinet, Mike hooked his thumbs into his jeans. It was a simple gesture; one she'd seen God alone knew how many times but right at that moment it became something else. It might have been the soothing heat of the water or the look in his eyes or everything all rolled into one, but looking up at him, all Claire could think was that she was naked, and he looked good too and his hands were right there.

Not very far away at all.

She remembered the feel of them, the feel of being beneath them. She imagined what it would be like to have his fingers in her hair, to be explored by a man who knew how to tease her until she wanted to scream. She imagined him naked too, with those arms wrapped around her and those hips, thrusting, thrusting, *thrusting* away.

Claire squirmed hard beneath the water, her thighs rubbing together in a not unpleasant way. She dropped her gaze. "I'm uh...I'm sorry to burst your bubble but uhmmm..."

The sentence didn't need finishing and she could see he knew it. Mike nodded, not looking away. "I know."

"Sorry."

"Don't be. We'll just have to make up for it another day." He smiled at her, and Claire blushed.

"You bet," she said and meant it.

Again, she thought he would leave and again he surprised her. He stepped closer, turned to face the sink and then slid down the wall 'til they were next to each other: one wet, the other dry. He propped his elbows on his knees and leaned his head back against the hideous floral wallpaper they'd meant to change since they moved in.

"You can go relax inside, you know. You don't have to sit with me. I don't want to keep you."

Mike shook his head. "I'm good here, if you don't mind the company."

She couldn't help pressing. "You sure you're all right, babe?"

The pause was telling but short of taking a crowbar to him she was out of options.

"Yeah, I'm all right. Just really tired."

Claire slipped an arm out of the water and intertwined her fingers with his. They sat together wordlessly for a time until, on the surface of the water, a bubble captured Claire's attention.

Chewing on her lower lip in concentration, she slowly snaked a hand along underneath. When she was in position, she pointed a finger skyward and skewered the bubble like a missile coming out of a silo. As soon as it popped, the thought came to her.

"Hey, you never answered my text before."

Mike gave her a blank look and then his features started working in tandem like circuits clicking. His eyes fluttered and his jaw shifted side to side. Finally it stopped and he blinked fully. "Sorry, I thought it was from...I got involved in...Never mind. Sorry."

"It's okay." She smirked knowingly and pointed at his pocket.

"It uhm..." He rubbed his stomach as though it pained him. "It died a while ago. The battery..."

Claire shrugged. "Mine's in the kitchen if you want to go grab it."

Dutifully, Mike creaked out of the room. He was back within a few seconds and seconds later the picture came to life.

Claire didn't know why her brain made the connection but looking at the sonogram always reminded her of a childhood art project. She could remember sitting in an oversized smock, scratching away at a black paint board and smiling as the colors beneath were revealed.

In the picture, etched out in long, jagged streaks of white, black and gray, Gabriel lay on his side, butt pointed out towards the world. Claire watched Mike smile in that warm way she always liked to see. She wanted to reach out and stroke his cheek, but she waited.

Underneath the photo, Claire's caption read, "*HE HAZ UR TUSHY!!!*"

Mike laughed so hard the back of his head bounced off the wall.

Claire, who'd never been one to let such a moment go by, giggled and pointed at him in a 'neener-neener' kind of way.

"Now...Now I'm really sorry I missed that," Mike finally choked out.

"Thought you'd like it."

By then the water had begun to cool so, stretching out her leg, Claire flipped the switch with her big toe. The water rushed down the drain with a sound like someone trying to whistle with their mouth full.

Keeping a tight grip on the handrails, and with a lot of groaning, Claire stood up. Mike held out an arm for her, but she waved him off. He settled for handing her a fresh towel and she smiled as little water drops cascaded off her belly. Wrapping herself quickly, she accepted another towel, with which she tied up her hair. As she put one foot out of the tub, Mike offered his hand again and this time she accepted. He used it as an anchor to pull her against him. Still dripping, Claire laid her head on his chest.

Standing there like that, she was sure Mike wouldn't be able to keep his hands to himself. The way he hugged her to him only made her think of his hands more. But though she was a bit disappointed when he didn't try anything, she couldn't really blame him.

Besides, the disappointment didn't last long. Soon after she blow-dried her hair, they went to bed. Claire settled onto her side and smiled as Mike crawled in a few seconds later. He encircled her in his arms and pressed his lips against the back of her head.

"Love you," he said quietly.

"Love you too."

Though she knew she would be up soon, whether for bathroom or baby or both, it no longer mattered to her. Pressed together like this, held so tightly, it was less than a minute before she was sound asleep.

The night passed quietly, and well.

Mike planted his elbows on either side of his keyboard. On the screen, a tiny hourglass spun in metronomic time while the hard drive whirred through its revolutions. Sitting next to him was a stack of mailed applications, fat envelopes taped shut against the press of the documents within. Every morning at nine thirty, the mail came in on a small pushcart driven by a stout, fiftyish woman whose name Mike never remembered.

Some mornings, he was lucky, and she only brought him a few. Today though, over a dozen landed on his desk with a heavy *thwack*. Some of them were filthy and dented, as if they'd been stepped on before arriving at his desk.

He'd nodded and signed his name onto the thick black plastic scanner she carried. It was company policy that every app be processed within one business day of receipt. Mike knew there was likely a reason for this, increased efficiencies or decreased turnaround time, but now he couldn't bring himself to care. The only thought which repeated itself as he picked up a letter opener was, *this is not my job*.

A year ago, all mailed applications were handled by Betty in Central Processing, a tiny, warm sweetheart of an octogenarian. Anyone who looked at her would have thought she was just an old woman who needed a reason to get out of the house. But those who shared an office with her knew she was one of the most competent workers the company had ever seen. Since she was rarely late and never disorganized, the company depended on her for any number of important daily tasks. And in true company fashion, rather than hire someone to replace her, they broke up her job piecemeal. Everyone remaining saw their workload triple overnight.

From over his shoulder came the jingle of Alma's many

bracelets approaching. There was a slight cant of gravity as she put a hand on his chair and leaned over.

"How many today?"

"Fourteen," he said, unable to keep the displeasure out of his voice. It took twenty minutes to process each application. That was on top of live customers, phone calls and updating Patrick's fucking spreadsheet.

"Lucky you," she said. Her head shook in the blue reflection of the screen. "Why did Betty have to go and retire?"

Mike shrugged. "She was eighty-four. I'd say it was about time."

"Oh, please. That woman was sprightlier than I am and I'm half her age."

Mike nodded. "Can't argue with you but I'll give you extra points for using 'sprightlier'."

She whapped his shoulder. "Don't start." Perching herself on the corner of his desk, she glanced carefully around the office then leaned in close, lowering her voice. "You made any plans yet?"

Mike didn't have to ask what she meant. Briefly he thought about lying, but his brain was still too overheated to come up with anything plausible. Instead, he shrugged and looked at her meaningfully.

Alma nodded, evidently finding the answer she was looking for. "Same here," she said quietly. "I can't remember the last time I updated my resumé. But a girlfriend said she could use some help with her daycare business. Just a few days a week."

"That's sounds good. At least it's something."

Alma rolled her eyes. "It's three days of screaming kids, poopy diapers and screaming kids."

Mike blinked at her. "Isn't that a little..."

"Shut up. I told her I'd think about it." Alma picked up one of the envelopes and gave it a squeeze as if testing it for ripeness.

Then threw it back down with a thud. "Seriously. How did this end up in your lap? I thought Pat was going to give this over to the people in Customer Service."

Mike sighed and punched the Enter key a few times, hoping it would light a fire under the main program which still hadn't loaded. "Apparently Customer Service bitched a blue streak and refused. Pat tried to pawn it off on Lauren, but..."

As one, they turned and stared at the empty desk in the corner.

"Is she even here today?" Alma asked.

"She's here. That's her stuff." A knockoff Gucci bag sat on the chair next to a stack of client files.

"And has anybody seen her since?"

Mike just gave her another look, setting his jaw. Alma shook her head, long braids swinging like black wind chimes.

"I swear to God, if that woman makes it to the new office and one of us doesn't..." Her fingers curled, nails digging into the back of Mike's chair.

"She won't make it," he said firmly, but Alma didn't look convinced. Her large, deep-set brown eyes glared at the faux Gucci.

"Then why haven't they fired her? If they're not thinking about keeping her, then why is she still here?"

Mike shrugged, his palms up. "Maybe they need the staff 'til the end." As Alma's eyebrows shot to ridiculous heights, Mike lowered his hands. "Okay, okay. You don't have to call me stupid so loudly."

Alma chuckled and pointed at the stack again. "Anything I can help with?"

He thought about it for a second, then turned to her. "Yeah, there is. Explain the whole 'I'm half her age thing' to me. Betty was eighty-four. The last time we cut cake for you, you said you were—"

*"Shut. Up. You."*

That got Mike laughing and though Alma tried to suppress a smile, she must have needed it as bad as he did because both caught the laughing bug. Others in the office looked on, questions in their eyes, but soon enough it infected them too.

Mike rolled his shoulders and patted the arm rests. For the moment, the pile in front of him didn't seem so terrible. He'd get through them and then he'd be home with his arm around Claire and they'd have a nice, quiet—

"Excuse me!"

Mike and Alma looked up. On the other side of the visitor's desk stood a man in his late sixties with unkempt brown hair and a face so wrinkled it looked like he'd spent the last ten years of his life sleeping outside.

"Yes, sir. Can we help you?" Mike heard himself ask.

The man's narrow shoulders shook, swaying his arms. "Yeah. I wanna sign up."

His words were short, indignant and pissed off. He slapped a beat-up leather valise on the desk and stared at them as if saying, *come on, hurry up.*

Alma looked the man up and down, then glanced at Mike, who nodded and flicked his fingers in her direction, their own signal that she could go, he'd handle it. Mike stood and walked over to the desk. "Sure, sir. I can help you."

"It's about time," the man said, even though Mike was sure he hadn't been standing there a minute ago.

The smell hit him when he was still five feet away. The man reeked of stale, cheap cigarettes, the kind they sell by the crate at highway gas stations. Mike tried breathing through his mouth, but the smell was so thick it had a taste to it.

Somehow, he still managed to be polite. "I just need to make a copy of your driver's license, sir and then we can get you started."

As the man reached into the back pocket of his jeans, Mike gave him a close once over. He was dressed in a heavy, black construction jacket with frayed sleeves over a faded plaid shirt. His jeans were caked with dirt and the wallet he pulled out was so packed with detritus Mike wondered how he could even sit on it. As the man flipped it open, Mike noted scraps of paper, old business cards, coupons and receipts before the license finally made an appearance. He held it up close to Mike's face, the surly expression in the photo a match for the one in real life.

"Thank you, sir." Mike reached out, being careful to keep his fingers as far away from the other man's as possible. The license felt old and gritty, filling him with the need to wash his hands the moment this was over.

Mike started to turn but the card slipped out of his hands. The man held it out still, expression unchanged. But when Mike reached for it again, he pulled it out of reach. Mike stared at him, the beginning of a new rock forming in his stomach.

"Sir?"

"I'm not giving you my license."

Somehow Mike managed to smile. "I'm afraid I need it for your application."

"I'm *not* giving you my license."

"O-kay. Why?"

"'Cause I don't give out my info. You don't need it. You saw my license, you know I have it." He waved it around like a backyard magician brandishing a wand at a kid's birthday party. *There it is. That's the trick. Now go eat cake.*

"Sir, I need to make a copy of your license and any insurance cards you're covered under."

"I'm not opening myself up to identity theft!"

"Identity-what? Sir, I—"

"I don't know what you'll do with it when you're out of my sight! You could leave my stuff lying around, somebody else could walk off with it." The man's voice was rising alarmingly and with every word the stench of cigarettes billowed forward.

"Sir, no one here is going to steal your identity. Everything we make a copy of is scanned in and then sent to the file room. Nothing gets left—"

"I'm not here to listen to you! I'm sick, you know? I've got problems you don't want to hear about. So stop talking to me about paperwork! I just want to apply for healthcare!"

"But to do that you need to give me your card."

It went on like that for several minutes. It vacillated between belligerence and exasperation, until the only thing left to say was said—

*"I wanna talk to your supervisor!"*

"You've got it, sir." Mike pointed to a chair, which the man took with a heavy sense of entitlement. Mike headed for Pat's office, threading through the arteries of desks. For some reason, he couldn't stop blinking. It wasn't to fight off tears—the heat in his eyes was dry and arid—but no matter where he looked, a white shadow would burst right in the center of his vision. Twice he almost walked into someone.

"Hey, what's going on?"

It was Margaret. She had a phone clutched between ear and shoulder, finger on the hold button.

"Just some crazy asshole losing what's left of his mind. He wants to talk to Pat."

"Don't bother."

Mike turned. He hadn't even seen Tom sitting there, tucked in the corner, two boxes of spreadsheet printouts between his knees.

"What?"

"I said don't bother."

"Why? Where is he?" Mike rapped out, hoping his tone would prove he didn't have time for crap.

"He's in his office."

Mike rolled his eyes and started walking again. "What? Is he in a meeting?"

"Nope, but you bother him and the joke's on you."

Hating himself just a little bit, Mike stopped again, blinking as several not quite unreasonable thoughts went to war in his head.

*Keep it together, he's still head of the section.*

*Do you honestly think he'll take you with him? He's worse than Pat!*

*You can't take the chance. You want to be part of the team or not?*

*I want to still be sane at the end of the day. But I don't think that's on the docket.*

"What joke?" he finally bit out, his fists bunching shakily at his sides.

Tom put one box to the side and looked at him. "Tell me something. If you were to walk into his office right now, what would you say to him?"

"That I've got an irate client who needs a supervisor to explain to him how he needs to follow the rules like everybody else."

Tom snorted so loudly he rocked in his seat. "Yeah, let me tell you how that's gonna go." He stood up and crossed his arms, leaning back on his heels. "You'll go in there and tell Pat there's a guy who needs to talk to him. Pat will say 'Sure, Mike, no problem. I'll be right out.'"

Mike almost laughed at Tom's spot-on impression of Pat's saccharine, brown-nosing voice.

"But you and I both know he'll leave you hanging for twenty minutes while that fuck out there stares holes through the back of your head. Then, two seconds after Pat comes out, the fuck will throw himself to the ground, practically pissing himself over how unfair we've been to him. It'll be a whole big production of 'woe is me.' Pat will listen for all of five minutes, then—and this is my favorite part—not only will he fold, but he'll also *apologize for you.* As if you're the one who was being a fuck. Now..." Leaning down, he put his face right in Mike's and grinned. "Tell me I'm wrong."

Mike opened his mouth, but no words came out. He closed it, then tried again but his brain was locked tight. He looked to Margaret for help, but she was already nodding, head slumped, eyes low. For a second, Mike looked past her to Pat's door which was closed, the plate which read 'Supervisor' looking dull and ineffectual.

Mike turned around and trudged back to his desk. The man...the fuck—Tom had called it right—had a cigarette clamped between his lips. He was hunched over in his chair, hands cupped in front of his face.

"Ah, there's no smoking in this building, sir!" Mike practically hollered, jumping at any opportunity to throw the man out of the building.

The fuck opened his hands, revealing nothing but his license. The sneer he conjured up made it clear Mike just lost fifty IQ points in his estimation.

Inwardly, Mike grimaced. "I've spoken with my supervisor sir, and he's decided to—"

"Yeah, I figured. Meanwhile I been sittin' here, wastin' more time."

"Yes, sir, I know. But you have to understand that I—"

"And I'm a sick man! I got problems. I'm entitled to treatment."

"Yes, sir. We're here to help you."

"Well, you're not helping me yet. So far, you've just been wastin' my time."

The muscles of Mike's stomach contracted, his face burned, and he tasted bile. "I'm sorry. Sir."

The fuck nodded and leaned back, suddenly at ease. He crossed one leg over the other and smiled, cigarette tilting up towards the ceiling. "Then let's get me signed up already."

Mike's whole body was so rigid, when he finally sat down, his back creaked like old floorboards.

The day did not improve.

Tom had just settled into his couch when the phone rang. He glanced at the display, smiled and let it ring. His belly was full, his ass comfortable and everything else had enough beer in it that the room rippled like a pond in a soft breeze.

The phone trilled twice more as he tilted his head back and took another deep swallow. On the fifth ring, half a second before the machine would pick up, he snatched the receiver and cradled it against his shoulder.

"Hey, sweets. You're lucky you caught me. I was in the bathroom, had to run to grab the phone."

Tom didn't even try to pretend like he was out of breath. His smile was a physical presence on the line.

"I'm so glad you made the effort, Tom." Linda said. Her voice was weary, as if it had walked every last mile from her phone to his.

Tom took another sip.

"So, what can I do for you, babe?"

"You were supposed to send over the rest of my things this morning. They're not here."

"I always said you had a keen sense of the obvious, babe."

"Don't call me 'babe.' I need the rest of my things, Tom."

"They're right where you left them. *Babe.* Come back home and you can have them."

"Please don't make this harder than it has to be, Tom. Please."

"I'm not making anything hard. You're the one who walked out. Means you're the one that has to come back and get 'em."

"I'm *not* coming back, Tom." The words twisted even as she said them.

Tom's smile widened and crackled with hoarfrost.

"There's a lot of clothes in those bags you left. You must be running low by now. That why you're calling me? 'Cause you're down to nothing but your skivvies?"

Linda's breath huffed on the line as if she'd squeezed it out of her lungs like a pastry bag.

"That's it, isn't it?" Tom cradled the beer bottle between his legs. The cold sent a not-unpleasant chill up his spine. "Tell me, what color are them skivvies?"

"Tom, this doesn't have to be like—"

"I'm betting it's those red frilly ones. You know. The ones that make your tits look bigger than they really are."

"Tom, for God's sake! Stop!"

"Stop what? I'm just sitting here thinking about my wife in her frilly nighty. It's not my fault. You should be here right now, babe. Not two states away with your sister. It's your fault I'm disappointed. Your fault you're upset. All of it. Your fault. So don't blame me."

He drained the last of his beer in a single swallow. The 'Aaah,' that escaped him was as satisfied as the growl of a bear in its cave. Still smiling, he listened to the choking gurgles his wife made.

Seconds passed, and then finally Linda sighed. She stretched it out 'til it was almost a word in itself.

"You're right, Tom. It *is* my fault."

Casually Tom put his feet up on the coffee table and crossed one ankle over the other.

"It's my fault we're apart. Just as it's my fault we were together in the first place."

He cocked his head to the side. "What?"

"Everyone warned me. Nobody liked you. Shit, my mother *hated* you. But me? I loved you. I loved the way you acted like you didn't give a shit. The way you could just say anything and get away with it. Even if you were wrong, even if it was hurtful."

"Babe, this isn't—"

"I even loved when you were angry with me! Isn't that a kick? The way you'd bristle and get ugly with me. That look you'd get. Oh God. I lost friends because of that look."

"Linda? What the fuck does this have to do with anything?"

"I'm just telling you what you want hear, dear. I'm admitting I'm wrong. It's my fault we got married. It's my fault I spent the last thirty-four years with a man who never once cared about me. A man who made me love him even when he bullied me. I had to run two states away before I could finally think straight."

"Linda. Shut the fuck up. Right now. Do not speak. *I* will tell you what you're going to do."

"That's another thing that's my fault, Tom! Oh yes, you hit it right on the head! Letting you make every decision for me. Where we lived, what we bought, who I talked to. I was so wrapped up, I couldn't even find the courage to talk to you about those magazines I found in your office last year!"

"Linda, I said shut the fuck—"

It took him a moment, but when he finally processed her words, something akin to a major systems failure occurred. Speech, cognitive processing, even eye-blinking froze. He could do nothing but listen.

"You know the ones I'm talking about don't you, *babe*? The

ones you keep in your desk? I was looking for something, I can't remember what, but hot damn, there they were! Page after glossy page of big, hairless *men* with tight asses and dicks like jumbo hotdogs."

Tom rattled like a car trying to turn over. His mouth moved but there was no sound.

"You know, once I found them, I had one of those stupid moments. You know what I mean, don't you? Where you can't figure out why you never figured it out before. All those years of you complaining about the light-in-the-loafers guys who lived across the street. Decades of you fucking me like you couldn't even spell vagina, let alone know what it was for. So, you know what, *babe?!*"

Something buried deep in Tom's hindbrain tried to prepare itself. There was a fusillade coming. Fléchettes would rend him if he didn't put on some fucking armor right this second.

But when the words came, they weren't anything he could have prepared for. Linda's voice, which had been rising by the second, suddenly halted where it was. A strange inflection, low and soft and compassionate, worked its way in.

"You need help, Tom. You need to talk to someone about..." She let out a long sigh. "I'm really not coming back, Tom. Can you understand that? Ever. I can't. This whole thing. You and me. It was broken from day one. Don't-Don't worry about my things. There's nothing there I really..." She cleared her throat. "Goodbye, Tom. I hope you... Get *help*, Tom. Goodbye."

When the line clicked, it pulled all the air out of the room. Not a sound, not even the beating of Tom's heart could be heard. It lasted exactly three seconds. The moment the dial tone kicked in, Tom exploded.

*"Fuck you, you goddamn whore bitch! I'll put my fuckin...You're gonna feel my dick all the way up your—"*

The bellow that followed was unintelligible. It was so filled with rage, so painful and animalistic that spittle flew from his throat as he roared. With both legs he kicked out as hard as he could, sending the coffee table tumbling. Jumping to his feet, he smashed the handset against a doorframe until it snapped in half.

He pitched the empty beer bottle at a table of family photos but missed by a foot. It bounced once then rolled gently into the kitchen, still whole. Spitting out a wordless stream of hate, Tom spun and drove his fist into the wall. The paint cracked but that wasn't enough. So he drove in again and again, trying for a space his whole arm could fit through.

On the fifth blow, something gave in his hand. A searing pain overtook him and raced all the way up his shoulder. Tom howled and reeled away from the stupid fucking wall that hurt him while Linda's words clanked and grated around in his head like loose parts.

Unthinking, needing a target for the shitstorm boiling within, the cross hairs in his head zoomed down on the coffee table. On its side the way it was, one leg was in the perfect position to send it flying.

Cradling his hand, Tom lined up and took two lumbering steps. *"Go fuck yourself!"*

The table was solid oak, each leg thicker than his calf. His bare foot connected and the crack that followed was the sound of three toes breaking in rapid succession.

Screaming, Tom hobbled about the room, searching for purchase. He used the wrong hand to steady himself against a wall and whimpered. His foot clipped the liquor cabinet and pain bore through him like a scabrous fist. It grabbed great handfuls of his guts and squeezed 'til he simply collapsed to the floor, back against the wall, head down and breathing slowly, praying he wouldn't be sick all over himself.

An entire forever passed. At least to him. His hand was like a baby's cry at three in the morning and his foot was a car fire burning like it would never go out. But the worst thing, the son of a bitchin' shit that really got to him, was the tears. He couldn't make them stop. They dripped down his face 'til he tasted nothing but salt.

"Pussy. Stop being such a fuckin' pussy."

Nothing helped but time. Eventually, as the minutes passed, he dried out. His breathing evened and the pain...shit, the pain was the same. But that didn't mean he had a choice about getting up.

With slow, agonizing jerks, Tom climbed to his feet. He leaned heavily against the wall, all his weight on one leg. He wiped his eyes and mouth, straightened his tie as best he could. He looked about the room and dejectedly shook his head. He wanted to see things in pieces. Photos torn, furniture ruined, fabric shredded. A trail of destruction leading to his feet that said *Stay away from that thing. It is not to be fucked with.*

But he found little evidence of his passing. The table was overturned but intact. The phone was ruined but he had a spare in one of the closets upstairs. And the hole that should have been in the wall was nothing more than a dent. A picture frame would conceal it easily.

A few minutes of cleanup and no one would ever know a man had erupted there at all.

Tom's leg was shaking, and his face burned. He hobbled towards the front door and twisted himself unnaturally to fish out his keys. Getting behind the wheel would be hard but he'd do it, no matter how much it hurt. He could still drive himself to the hospital. That much he was capable of, at least.

*"Goddamn sonofabitch!"*

The wind whistled through the open window, flattening Mike's hair against his skull as he drove.

"Come out of nowhere and treat me like shit? Fuck you!"

He'd opened the window hoping the freezing night air would calm him, kill the fire in his chest. But instead, it did the opposite. He was pushing eighty on the Northern State, every inch of him alight as trees and parkway signs flew by.

Mike stretched out his voice into a high, prissy whine. "I'm sick! I got problems!"

Then he punched it down into a low, 'Father Knows Best' baritone. "Well, I guess now you know what living under a bridge for twenty years will do to you, dontcha you little fuck!"

Mike's fingers wrapped so tight around the steering wheel, his forearms ached. He screamed at the wheel and pounded the dash, all while hoping to reach his limit. But the more he gave into that ugly, hateful thing, the more it grew within him.

"'Let me tell you how this is gonna go.' No, Tom! No! Let me fucking tell *you*!"

Each new word he threw out into the night scoured his throat as if it was stripping away layers of him to make room for something new and horribly different. Too far recessed into the dash for his fists to reach, the clock blinked, and Mike gritted his teeth. Fifteen minutes from home. Less than that if he kept at this speed.

He shook his head rapidly and tried to think of somewhere he could go, an out of the way place where he could drive and scream 'til the anger died away, or his voice broke, whichever came first. He couldn't let Claire see him like this. He'd frighten her and that would be too much to bear in one day. No, a side trip was better, one that would give a few minutes to duct tape himself back together. But where the fuck could he—

He came roaring up on them before he knew what was happening.

Two cars were stopped dead in the middle of the road, canted sideways like broken sentries still trying to guard the overpass behind them. Front ends smashed, bumpers twisted, the blacktop glittering with the flash of broken glass and the spark of road flares.

Mike lost a second in the glittering, but the man tore him out of it. The man standing in the space between the cars, both arms waving, flashlight in each hand.

Screaming, Mike stomped the brake, but it was slow, so terribly, awfully slow. The car shuddered, wheels shrieking against the road. Mike strangled the wheel, but there was nowhere to go. To his left loomed the divider, the kind of thing that repelled semis. To his right nothing but trees and now the man's arms were trembling, his eyes panicky wide. He was thirty feet from Mike's front end and in seconds he'd be nothing but broken pieces flying back through...

...The gap, the space between the cars. There wasn't time to guess, Mike just jerked the wheel and prayed. Fifteen feet out and his heart convulsed painfully, shaking his chest like a struck bell. The man glowed in the headlights, mouth falling open, the terror hitting him too late.

Mike wanted to wave him off, but his hands were fastened to the wheel.

Ten feet and the world was down to the slowly dropping needle, the whoosh of Mike's tires. He knew it would work and he knew it wouldn't. It was all too fast. Much too fast.

The man finally moved, flashlights dropping, body diving to the right. Mike bawled fiercely. *God help me.*

The man's shoes sailed past Mike's windshield. The cracked cars flew by so close they should have traded paint. Mike's breath wheezed and his head pounded but in half a second he was through, engine still roaring, tires gnashing the road ahead.

Blinking dazedly, Mike kept going. His instincts dragged his foot from brake to gas. Without thought he reeled towards the next exit, cutting into the turn, almost making the Explorer fishtail. At the bottom of the ramp he bounced across two lanes and into a gas station at the corner.

He pulled up to the first pump even though it was on the opposite side of the gas tank. He was shaking. Badly.

*God in heaven, I almost...*

Laying his head against the wheel, Mike squeezed his eyes shut. His legs wouldn't stop bouncing and a severe chill rocketed up into his chest. It took real effort to pry his fingers off the wheel.

The wind, which he'd hoped would calm him before, was so cold now it tightened the skin of his face 'til it ached. But it failed to stop his brain from making him relive the moment at a thousand thoughts a second.

*I almost killed a man.*

*I could have died.*

*I hit him.*

*No! I didn't, I'd have felt it.*

*Would you?*

*Yes!*

*You're wrong.*

*No! I didn't hit him. I know it!*

He threw open the door before he'd even taken off his seatbelt. He railed against it, tried to rip it from the mount, before finally punching the button. Out of the car the cold was like steel, hard and sharp and burning him harshly with every breath. He shivered as he moved around the truck, gray clouds of breath trailing in his wake. He looked at the car from every angle and bent close 'til his nose was inches away.

Nothing.

No dents, scrapes or stripped paint. No *blood* or broken pieces. Only Mike with his hands flat on the hood, fingers splayed, fighting the urge to vomit.

*The house. My job. The baby. My son. If I'd hit that man...*

*I didn't hit him!*

*If you had...*

*There's no damage. None. He's fine. Everything's fine.*

*You could have lost everything!*

It nearly overcame him. His stomach lurched as rancid chunks filled his throat, but he swallowed hard. Then again. The taste in his mouth didn't bear thinking about but he shoved it down and kept it there.

He sucked in air deep and slow, 'til the shaking finally passed. Straightening painfully, he heard his back crack even over the wind. For the first time since he pulled in, he looked around. His was the only car under the bright halogen lights. Odd for this time of night, but Mike silently thanked God for it all the same.

Beyond the reach of the lights, the trees were so black and barren they looked as if a child had drawn them with permanent marker. Hanging before them, the gas price signs were glaringly white, and the burning smell of gasoline crawled its way into Mike's lungs.

Across the lot, the clerk watched him through the convenience store window. Amid cartons of cigarettes and scratch-off tickets he glared at Mike with wary concern. His hand was very close to the telephone.

Quickly, Mike built something close to a smile and affixed it to his face. He waved jerkily.

*I'm fine, sir. Not dangerous at all, I swear. Just a guy stopping in to check under the hood for body parts.*

He bought four dollars' worth of gas and drove away as fast

as he could, praying it didn't look like he was running. Back on the road, he was shocked that only ten minutes had passed.

Right then, staring glassily at the road, his thoughts about the fuck were more distant than the miles behind him. He stuck to a decent speed the rest of the way home. He wasn't even that late when he finally pulled into the drive.

Twisting the key, he left the radio alive. He nestled his head against the window and closed his eyes. Ten Thousand Maniacs sang about lovers and the night and who belonged to whom. It was the live version, the only one the radio played. As the last note played, an audience more than twenty years dispersed clapped and cheered. This too faded out, replaced instantly by drums and fanfare. A chorus of voices blasted out.

*Ninety-seven point five! W-A-L-K Wea-Ther! Good evening, everybody! This is your Walk Traffic and Weather, brought to you by Walmart. Walmart! Home of the savings! Well, it looks like the storm we've been dreading all week is not going away. We're talking about at least a foot of snow, maybe even two feet so be sure to stock up before—*

Mike twisted the key that last inch. In a way, the silence that followed was worse than the peppy doom and gloom. Without it there was nothing to distract him from his overclocked brain except the beat-to-shit phone sitting next to him on the seat.

Glancing at it he cringed, heart sinking into a black fog. Lights from the neighbor's house twinkled in the spider web fractures on the screen, highlighting them in yellow and white. *Three, maybe four hundred at least. You're not even halfway through your contract and you never got insurance on it. Why bother? It would have been just more money thrown out the window. Besides, you're always so careful.*

Mike ran his thumb over the screen. The spiteful, unvarnished voice in his head was almost disappointed it hadn't snapped in half. For no other reason than just because, he held down the power button for a three count. He was honestly shocked when the maimed thing flashed to life.

The screen rippled as though it were a puddle of water. It even chimed normally. Within a few seconds, Mike was staring at his home screen with the icon for one missed call highlighted. With the night around him and figures from his bank accounts tallying up in his head, Mike remembered an article he'd come across last year during a rare break on the job.

It'd been about a group of snowboarders out on the slopes, doing stunts for no one else's benefit except their own, when an avalanche swallowed them whole. It threw them, rolled them and swung them sideways so many times they couldn't tell up from down. No matter which way they turned, the world looked the same.

Right then, Mike couldn't tell if he was looking down or up, hoping to see a connection to the world.

Nothing he did caused the screen to react. The icons were as immovable as paintings.

Mike stuffed the phone back in his pocket and popped open the door. Winter assaulted him on the walkway, but he forced himself to move easily, not tense up. By the time he slipped the key in the lock there was a smile on his face. He used all that tension to keep it there. *That's the way a man walks in the door.*

Inside was warm and bright and that first breath of home was so goddamn good.

Mike slammed the door behind him and just breathed, taking a few precious seconds to push everything else aside. But no matter how hard he tried, his memories, filled to the brim with fear, were stronger than he was.

He found Claire in her favorite spot. She had her afghan across her knees and a bowl of pretzels balanced on her belly. She was staring intently at something on the TV.

"Hey babe," she said, waving but not looking up.

"Hey, love." Mike dropped his things by the door.

"How was your day?" She was watching Rachel Ray. Her eyes were glued to the celebrity chef's hands as she put together a dish that looked big enough to feed a family of eight.

"Oh fine," he said, as happily as he could fake.

She looked up, lips forming for a kiss. "Glad to hear—"

She paled. Her eyes widened and she put a hand over her heart.

*"What's wrong?"*

Mike was taken aback. He struggled for words while barely able to hold her gaze. "What do you mean?"

"You...You look..."

"I'm fine, babe. Nothing's wrong." He put both hands on her shoulders and kissed her forehead. "It's just been a long day. I missed you."

"No. No, no, no. People don't look like that after a 'long' day."

"Babe, I'm fine really."

"Mike talk to me, okay? Stop looking at me like that, you're scaring me."

Mike realized he was still smiling. He'd forgotten to stop, and it took him a second too long to correct. "I'm...I'm okay. It's just been..."

"Sit."

"Babe, really. I'm goi—"

"Mike for Christ's sake, sit down before you fall down!"

He sat and it was only after the cushion took his weight that he really felt it. The heaviness of exhaustion. The small white shadows flickering in his vision. The way his brain threatened to stall every time he blinked.

She looked at him searchingly. "Talk to me, hon. What happened today?"

He almost laughed. Telling her about today wouldn't even

scratch the surface. The whole week was eating at him, and the week wasn't even over yet. What would telling her about today do? It wouldn't even...he looked at his wife.

She was leaning towards him, hair pulled back almost painfully tight. Worry and fatigue were squeezed into every line of her face. She had the look of a long-distance runner on her last lap. Weary beyond measure but determined. So determined to keep going. Telling her about today wouldn't cover the entire terrain of his problems. But it might cover *enough*.

He broke off a few pieces of his week and laid them out for her. Tom's put-downs and constant pressure, Jerry and his bullshit, and even that the office was moving. But no further. He drew a line and stuck to it. He watched Claire mull over everything the way she always did. She asked for details about what Jerry said. Asked questions he hadn't even thought of, in fact. It went on for ten minutes.

"Okay. Well, paying off the Explorer is out, we both know that. You'd think Jerry would know that too, with all the paperwork we sent him."

This time when Mike laughed it was real. "That's just what I thought."

She didn't smile, too deep in thought. But she did take his hand, rub her thumb across his knuckles. "I know we worry about how much money we have. But look. We've got enough to pay the mortgage for the next six months before we have to either dig through the couch for change or sell one of our kidneys. That's enough time for us to figure something out."

Outwardly Mike nodded while inwardly he shook his head. How could the woman who was complaining about dinner yesterday be the one to calm him down tonight? "Yeah, of course we can," he said, though he didn't believe a word of it. "There's got to be..."

"What town is your office moving to?"

"What?"

She stared at him, her features drawing down into a *'Come on, keep up.'*

He could feel the gears in his head going into overdrive, trying to remember. "Um, I-I think...I think they said Farmingdale."

Claire nodded, visibly perking up. "Okay, okay we could work with that. I used to live in Farmingdale, all the major bus lines stop there, and the train isn't hard to get to. Where is the office? What's the address?"

Mike ran to get his notebook out of his briefcase. The more Claire talked, the more animated she became. It was an infectious energy and though he still had no idea where she was going with this, he was too invested to stop. He gave her the address and she jumped on Google. In less than a minute, she was pointing excitedly at a map.

"Okay, look. Your new place is here. The train station is just a few blocks away. They run every hour during the week. You could walk there no problem."

"I guess, sure. But how much could that really save us on gas?"

She gave him an exasperated look. "Babe, I'm not talking about gas. I'm talking about selling the Explorer."

He blinked. His mouth opened and closed while his brain tried to hurdle a roadblock. "What? But...What about—"

"What about what? Think about it, babe. It costs you something like fifty bucks to fill up the tank, right? If we sold the Explorer, that's money we can put in our pocket every week along with everything we'd save on maintenance and insurance. I mean we've got two cars and one barely leaves the driveway. What do we really need the Explorer for?"

"What about shopping trips? Or if we want to go out for a night?"

"We've still got the Corolla, it's not like we'll be marooned. Besides the supermarket is just up the road. We could walk there in ten minutes. As for nights out, come on babe." She pointed at her stomach. "We're not going to have any nights out for a *long time*."

"What if the Corolla craps out, or there's an emergency?"

"That's why God invented ambulances. Babe, we can do this. It might not be a permanent solution but at least it will buy us more time. Once Gabriel's born, maybe I can do some tutoring part time. There's lots of young kids in this neighborhood, I'm sure some of them have parents who'd like them to pass math."

Mike laughed and shook his head. He could see the logic of it, but he still didn't like it. The Explorer was the first new car he'd ever owned, and they still owed money on it. They'd get some of it back but...It was his first new car. Bought during the days when they both worked, and they had a lot more money and less worries and they'd just been happier.

Claire reached out and brushed her fingers along his cheek. "Look, babe. We need to do this. We're out of choices. I know there's a lot we've been talking about doing. A lot of stuff we should have started already." She took a deep breath, marshalling herself. "I don't think either of us every really wanted to admit how bad things were getting."

Mike shook his head. "We went to the bank for a loan. We've looked at options and—"

"But we never talked about what else we should be doing! We applied for the loan, and then what? Did we talk about what we'd do if we got denied? Did we talk about me getting another job after the baby is born? I mean, shit, we still haven't figured out what we're going to do about daycare!"

Mike tried to think of something to say but his head was too full of her questions.

"I know you and I are stubborn people from a long line of stubborn people and sometimes, that's not a bad thing. But for the last few months we've been talking about literally everything else except what we need to. We can't afford to be the kind of people who would rather tear themselves in half than talk about what we're carrying. It damn near broke my parents more than once and you can't tell me it wasn't the same for yours."

She held out her hands, though whether in entreaty or to stave off his defense he couldn't be sure.

"I don't want to see that happen to us. To *you*. The stress is killing both of us and I can't keep watching you walk in the door every day like you're dying by inches. You're too important to me. I just...I want you to know that you can talk to me."

Mike wasn't fully conscious of it at first. The sound seemed to come from a place just past the corner of his eyes and when he finally found it, he tried with everything he had to stave it off, but it wasn't enough.

The noises he made were ruined things cobbled together from constant headaches and sleeplessness and exhaustion.

"I'm...I'm sorry," he choked out, tears pouring, nose stuffed to the brim.

"What are you apologizing for?"

"I just...you've got... Y-you've got so much you're dealing with. And I never wanted to add to what you're—"

"Babe." Claire cupped his chin and lifted 'til they were eye to eye. "Look, I know I've had to leave you with a lot lately and for that I'm the one who should be sorry. You take care of me but you're not alone in this, okay? You can still come to me. I want you to come to me, you know. Vent, bitch, cry if you need to. I can't do much around here, but I can keep you from driving yourself crazy. If you'll let me."

Mike's body didn't so much as relax as melt. His breath

hitched and he held on to her as tightly as she was holding onto him.

Eventually though, little things intruded, as they were wont to do. The pretzel bowl was in danger of spilling off the couch. Claire plucked it up and set it on the end table, flicking salt off her fingers. The timer on the oven went off and they stood slowly, arm in arm.

"Soup's on," she said with a half-smile.

Mike leaned on her as they shuffled into the kitchen and was surprised at how easily she carried his weight. Despite everything, Claire never so much as wobbled. Her head remained high, her shoulders square and the arm she wrapped around his waist was strong. Glancing at her, Mike, who up 'til this point had imagined himself the cavalry, now felt like a green private being borne off the battlefield by the sergeant-at-arms.

"So, dare I ask if anything good happened today?" she asked as he sat at the table.

Mike shook his head as if it were the heaviest thing in the world and Claire hugged him tight. He kissed her cheek and tucked his face into her hair. He felt her ribs press into the soft flesh of his arms as she took a deep breath. She held it for a long moment, the center of her so expanded Mike heard her heart thrum as though it were being pressurized.

"I love you," he whispered.

"I love you too, babe."

Baked ravioli came out of the oven, filling the house with the scents of gooey melted cheese and bubbling tomato sauce. She dished out heaping portions for them, then sat down. She had the fork halfway to her mouth when she paused.

"Oh hey, I forgot. Did you ever grab the Tylenol on your way home?"

He froze mid-chew. All the bits and pieces he'd left out

squirmed like slugs in his chest. His eyes were so dried out they hurt every time he blinked. His nose was clogged, his back ached and even the ravioli wasn't enough to get rid of the salty, phlegmy taste of his breakdown. No, no more tonight. Another confession would only break him beyond repair.

The lie took forever to gather steam in his brain but if Claire noticed, she gave no sign.

"Sorry, babe. I forgot. I'll pick it up tomorrow."

Mike chewed mechanically and waited.

"Okay. No biggie," she said at last, shrugging.

"I'm sorry." He hated saying it again, but even this was another mark on the growing list of wrong things in his head.

"Babe, I said don't worry about it. Really. I can pick it up at the store tomorrow."

She said it like she meant it, but he couldn't help watching the way she grimaced as she shifted in her seat. Tylenol was the only thing that helped with the pain. He tried to go back to eating but the food had lost its flavor. Each bite sat like a brick in his stomach though he kept at it, chewing mechanically, praying to recapture the good feeling they'd had such a short time ago.

---

"I got in a fight."

The woman at reception blinked slowly, as though processing Tom's words one at a time.

"All righty, sir, that's not a problem. Have you ever been seen here before?"

"Yeah." He pressed his license and insurance cards into a doughy hand. This Urgent Care Clinic was less than half a mile from his house which put it five and a half miles closer than the nearest hospital. It was only an hour before they closed but the waiting area still teemed with sweating teenagers, people hacking into surgical masks and one guy who gave every indication that his ass *really* fucking hurt.

With a practiced boredom, the receptionist placed a clipboard on the counter. "Fill these out and bring them back up when you're done."

Tom held up his hand. It was twice its normal size and the reddish pink of an overstuffed sausage.

She blinked once and nodded at him. "I'll be right back." Her smile was meaninglessly professional.

Looking at her, Tom thought of a hairless bloodhound. She was painfully pale and had thick rolls of skin jiggling about her neck and chin. When she came back, she sported his cards, the clipboard, a shiny new wheelchair and a bag of ice.

"Let's get you patched up."

A nurse rolled him down the hall while the receptionist peppered him with questions. Name, social, birthdate, emergency contact...When he said none they rolled to a stop and the two women looked at each other. Tom gritted his teeth.

"Are you sure?" The receptionist asked, her personality softening for the first time. "We like to have the name of somebody who can come and get you, should you need it."

Tom pressed down on the ice and refused to look at either of them. "I'm sure."

Another shared glance. The nurse leaned around 'til she could look at Tom full on. "It doesn't have to be a relative. If you've got a good friend—"

Tom shook his head hard. No way did he want Jimmy seeing him like this. His pride would never survive the call. Better to deal with it on his own. Anything else would just cause more problems than he already had.

"I said I'm sure. Can we get going now? I'm hurtin' here."

The nurse was a blonde, fortyish blur in the corner of his eye. "Mr. Downes, we would really prefer to have—"

Tom planted his hands on the armrests like he was going to propel himself out of the chair. "Fuck it, never mind. Maybe they won't give me this kinda shit at St. Joseph's."

The nurse dropped a surprisingly strong hand on his shoulder. Which was good because with the pain he was in, Tom doubted he could've made it to the door let alone his car.

"There's no call for that kind of language, Mr. Downes. We're just trying to help you."

The nurse straightened and they started rolling again. On another night Tom might have smirked. He loved it when people said things like 'that kind of language.' As if there was any other way to describe what he was going through. But tonight he didn't even have the energy for little victories. He sat quietly, grateful to have somebody else doing the driving.

They brought him into one of the exam rooms and plugged his vitals into a computer. The X-Rays themselves were painless but he almost whimpered when they took off his shoe. A few minutes of alone time later and a thin Indian man in a dark blue turban swept in.

"You look like you've been through it tonight, my friend."

Tom didn't even try to pronounce the doc's name. The man's accent was thick, but his English was textbook quality. He smiled confidently at Tom through a beard as black as the night sky.

Tom nodded tiredly at him while he rolled over a stool. "You got that right."

"How did it happen?"

Tom shrugged. "Couple guys shooting their mouths off at the bar. I got into it with 'em and it went sideways faster than I thought."

The doc worked him over with single-minded efficiency, prodding at hand and foot 'til Tom had to bite his lip to keep from kicking him in the face.

"It has been a while since I've treated a bar room injury. I hope I remember how to handle it. The police can be quite particular about their reports."

Tom froze.

"I, uh. I never filed a report."

The doc lifted a neatly trimmed eyebrow at him though there wasn't an ounce of surprise on his face. "Oh? Why not?"

"It...wasn't nothing, really. No big deal. I handled it."

Quick black eyes watched him carefully. It wasn't a hard stare, but it clearly said that the man's bullshit detector was in perfect working order.

"Maybe the bar owner called the police. If you and your friends broke anything he may have been inclined to—"

"*No.* No, we didn't. I uh..." Tom tried not to squirm. "I slipped him some cash on the way out. For, you know, for the trouble. And they weren't my friends."

Tom's armpits were damp, and his shirt clung to his back. Every time he breathed that goddamn wetness bubbled in his lungs.

The wheels of the doc's stool squealed as he rolled over to the computer. A couple of keystrokes later and Tom's x-rays appeared on the screen. He studied them silently for a minute and then sighed. Tom never knew he could hate a sound as much as he did right then.

"Well, my friend, you're definitely messed up, that's for sure."

"Really? Ain't that a kick?"

The doc continued as if he hadn't spoken. "Your toes are fractured but they seem stable. We can tape them together and I will fit you with a brace before you leave. It'll take some of the pressure off while the bones heal."

He flicked a glance at Tom. "Your fingers, however, are not

so stable. I'll give you splints for now but if they don't heal properly, you may need surgery to correct them."

A chill swept through Tom at the thought of surgery. He was a week and a half away from finding out if he still had a job or not. If he needed surgery and his insurance ran out...

*You don't mind being crippled do you, troop?*

Wheeling back over, the doc steepled his fingers and pointed them at him. "Do I need to tell you to follow up with your doctor in the morning?"

Tom shook his head and the doc smiled.

"Good. I'm glad to hear it. Now you're going to want to watch out for any signs of redness. Keep up with the ice every hour for the next day or until the swelling goes down. But don't leave it on for more than twenty minutes. If you start to feel any numbness, *call your doctor immediately*. Do you understand?"

A part of Tom wanted to give him a bullshit answer, to cover up the shit-scared voice in his head. But between the pain, the embarrassment and the doc's no bullshit stare, he was drained to the dregs. All he could do was blink and nod silently while the doc went to work on him.

Tape, gauze and splints all came and went and maybe it was the calm way the doc went about it, but as the minutes passed Tom's focus drifted 'til he was staring stupidly.

It was the doc's hands. They were the problem, and he couldn't believe he never noticed it before. They moved like master crafted machines. Precise and smooth, not a hint of shudder. They were the wrong color and far too hairy but still, without meaning to, he connected them to another pair of hands now forty years past.

Wiesbaden Army Airfield in Germany. He'd been twenty years old and as young and dumb and full of cum as Johnny Utah. Just a young clerk sitting in the infirmary, cradling what he hoped wasn't a broken hand. The nurse sat him down and left him to stew about what came next. He'd just finished worrying for the eighth time how this would look in his file when the doc came in.

"What's up, troop? How you feeling?"

The man was big, and Tom could say that cause he was six feet himself and even sitting down, the guy would've towered over him.

He had groomed brown hair, a solid build and arms that looked long enough to shake Tom's hand from the doorway. He smiled as if the two of them were already friends, making Tom both relax and tense up at the same time. The beat of his heart felt funny too. Faster than it should've been.

Tom noted the lieutenant's bars on his lab coat and made to salute.

"Save it, private. There's nothing weirder than a guy saluting you in a hospital gown."

Tom dropped the hand, felt a heat creep up his neck. But the doc, Marc Richards by his nametag, just laughed it away.

"Come on. Let's see what you've done to yourself."

The exam was quick but exhaustive. Richards checked Tom's hand, turned it this way and that. It hurt but Tom was surprised to find he didn't mind. The surety with which Richards moved was comforting. As if he knew exactly what he was doing every minute of the day.

After fifteen minutes, Richards wheeled over a stool and sat down. He fished a pack of Marlboro Reds out of his pocket and stuck one between his lips. A second one appeared, and Tom accepted it gratefully.

Crumpling the now empty pack, Richards tossed it dead on perfect across the room into the waste basket. The spark of a lighter, and the room filled with two drifting contrails of smoke.

"Well," Richards said between drags. "It's not broken."

Tom sighed and leaned back a little.

"But that ain't the important thing," Richards went on. He pointed two fingers at Tom's puzzled expression. "The important thing is how it happened. So spill."

Tom shifted on the table, cast his eyes left and right. "I was working in the supply room with Phillips, my squad mate. We'd finished inventory and there was nothing to do but stand there and smoke, y'know?"

Richards nodded.

"Right. So, we're standing there like a couple a dicks, and he just starts whistling. And not like songs or anything. Not even in tune. Just whistling, 'cause he could for over an hour, and it was driving me fuckin' nuts. I kept telling him to knock it off, but he just smiled and kept at it."

Richards tapped ash onto the floor. "Yeah, he sounds like a fuck."

Emboldened, Tom thrust out his cigarette like he was impaling Phillips. "Damn right. Anyway, he keeps going on and I keep trying to tell him I'm gonna lay him out. But he just keeps smiling. So finally, I just couldn't take it anymore."

"Did you lay him out?"

"Yeah, but...I also kinda hit his helmet."

Richards snorted. "Yeah, that'll about do it. You're lucky you *didn't* break your hand."

Tom nodded and kept his head low. He looked up at Richards nervously. "So. Does this uh. Does this have to go in my file, lieutenant?"

Richards didn't answer at first. He watched Tom with closed, crafty eyes and let the seconds tick past. He took a last couple drags on his smoke, right down to the filter, then ground it out beneath his shoe.

"I have to put something in, just to explain the injury. But..."

Another firm, steady gaze.

"I'll tell you what. There are a couple of Air Force boys

here, flying out of the air strip today. I'll put in that you got into a fight with one of those fucks. Captain can't stand the Air Force commander. He'll yell at you 'cause he has to, but he'll respect you for it too. Especially if you make a point of telling him you knocked him down in one punch."

Tom smiled and dragged the last bit of smoke out of his cigarette. He crushed it between two fingers. "Thanks, lieutenant. This means a lot to me."

Richards stood and raised his eyebrows. "Oh, I didn't do this for free, private. You owe me a beer."

Tom laughed. "Next time we're on leave. You got it."

"I'll hold you to that. Leave's coming up next month."

Tom remembered being excited then, though he never wanted to question why. He only knew he couldn't wait to get off the base for a little while, away from the shit food, and the hundred or so guys who didn't know what a shower was for. Away from all the hurry up and wait.

He didn't have a lot of clear memories of that night. He remembered the two of them leaving the base and walking into this giant beer hall, laughing about something over the first round. But after that, the world went for a swim. He didn't have a fucking clue how many halls they went to or how much they drank. He couldn't even remember where they met the girls.

In one memory, it was just him and the doc, and in the next they each had an arm around something warm and soft and female. It was like a film with reels missing.

Tom's girl was short, wheat-haired and curvy. Richards' was...also blonde? Dirty blonde, maybe? Fuck it, not important. What mattered was that neither of them spoke much English but 'soldier,' 'beer' and 'American' proved to be enough.

A few lost reels more and it was late, or early and they were all in somebody's bedroom. Tom was on the bed with his blonde on her back, her head slamming a foot from the edge of the mattress, the doc sat in a chair in the corner facing the bed, the other blonde straddling his lap.

It could have been the beer or that they were all in it together bucking away, but the whole thing was more than real in a way. The bitter and hoppy scent of the blonde's breadth in his face as he got into a rhythm, the sweet feel of her tit in his hand. The way the other blonde moaned as she cow-girled Richards.

Combined with the missing reel feeling, sensory memories created a strobe effect in Tom's head. Each flash was something different, but it was all connected, all the same story.

The blonde's yelps as Tom pounded away, the other blonde's ass rippling as she rode doc like God's own little piece. Richards' large, strong hands tugged on the other blonde's hair. The smell of hops and musk and pussy was in the air around them.

Tom remembered Richards staring at him over the other blonde's shoulder, eyes steady and simmering. The heat in them rose towards something Tom felt all the way down in the bottom of his balls.

A sudden switch, another missing reel, the other blonde on her knees, draped forward over the bed. The two blonde's faces were inches apart, their cries like the riffs of bass and guitar. Richards was there, behind the other blonde, only a few feet away. Tom pounded his girl good, but his eyes were nowhere near her, the two of them, Tom and the doc, their eyes locked, pumping away harder than ever. They went 'til Tom's lungs couldn't pull in air fast enough, 'til his whole body trembled and sweat slicked him from toes to crown.

He groaned like he was in pain, saw the muscles in Richard's chest tighten, and then suddenly he was gone, hit by something bigger than him, bigger than anything he'd ever met in his life. It took hold of him, drained him and wrung him out, left him weakened, but filled with a heavy light.

He barely registered the blonde's shrieks as she came. He heard doc's shout as clear as gunfire outside his window.

They all collapsed, and the bed creaked like it would break. The girls murmured things neither of them understood. Doc smiled at him and gave a thumbs-up. After that, the rest of the night died away to him, leaving not even an echo. He woke up the next day with his balls so drained it was a pleasure that almost hurt.

As he hobbled into his bedroom, older, patched-up Tom tried to keep his chin up, but it was a tough hill to climb. His index and middle fingers were splinted and the boot the doc gave him threw off his gait. In his pocket was a brand spanking new bottle of painkillers he'd been lucky to get, and instructions on how to shower with all the new hardware.

He groaned aloud as he sat, so tired it felt like weights were attached to his eyelids. And though his body probably could've fallen asleep where he was, Tom's mind was still dancing like a college kid around a bonfire. In the center of the flames were memories of Germany and Linda and what it all meant, but the kid in him wouldn't stop. He went right on leaping and jumping with his back to the heat.

*So what?* the kid asked. *So what if Linda found the mags? So what if it was hard to fuck without thinking about that night? That's not my fault. You know whose fault it is though, don'tcha?*

The more the kid talked, the more Tom liked what he heard. Maybe if Linda had been better between the sheets, he wouldn't have had to think about that night so much. How many years had it been since she *really* put her back into it? Fucking forever, that's how long. And she thought he was the one who didn't know how to fuck? Christ!

He'd banged her sagging ass for years. He was bored. It was the same with the magazines. He wasn't a goddamn faggot. He needed something different every once in a while, that's all. There was nothing wrong with it, and he goddamn sure as shit didn't need anybody's fuckin' help.

It took some work to open the pack of pain killers, even just holding them steady sent embers of pain all the way up his wrist. But in a minute or two, a couple of Oxy went down with a glug and he stretched out across the bed. Fuck the covers, they could stay where they were.

With his head deep in a pillow, a dusty, ash-colored version of the rage he'd felt earlier came back. It settled right next to him, and he stared at his wedding photos. Looked long and hard at the cunt who told him he needed help.

Tom let the rage go where it wanted while deep inside, the Oxy circled the perimeter before charging in. At the center, at home in his head, he closed his eyes and smiled. He was back in that bedroom in Germany only this time it was Linda beneath him. Crying out, calling his name, telling him she was so sorry while he drilled away like he was aiming for the floor.

Richards was there, too. Of course he was. He wouldn't be anywhere else. Not with those eyes and shoulders and stomach and hips and how he was cheering for Tom to give it to her like he owned her.

The day had not been kind but none of it stopped him. He still stood up tall and once he started stroking, the spasms swept away everything he had left. They emptied him of every care for Linda or the bills or surgery or even the fucks at work. He crumpled them up, all those shitty worries, and threw them away. Because, at least for the moment, he was free.

The rest could go fuck itself.

*Jesus Christ. He scared the Hell out of me.*

Claire sat very still, dinner and the dishes forgotten. Being careful not to turn her head, she kept the hall doorway in her peripheral vision. She needed to be sure where Mike was without making it look obvious. It wasn't that she was afraid of him. Claire couldn't imagine a life where she might be afraid of her husband.

When she'd seen Mike's tears her heart broke, but in a strange, jagged, guilty way it made her feel better. She'd wanted to get past the silences and the don't-worry-about-its for longer than she was comfortable remembering. And though everything Mike told her made her want to cry along with him, it had been a relief to finally talk about it all.

But now that the moment had passed, she was left alone with the fear she'd been fighting since he walked in the door. By distracted degrees she became aware of her thumb and the rough, jerky revolutions it made against her wrist. Glancing down, she gasped quietly.

The skin was as red as a cherry tomato and the veins, drawn out by friction, looked unhealthy and far too pronounced. A long angry scratch arced down from the heel of her palm and the fact that it didn't hurt only made it worse in a way Claire couldn't explain, even to herself.

Flinging her hands apart like they were two squabbling kids, she tried to think of nothing. To just sit there until she no longer remembered what scared her in the first place. But her fear simply circled back around 'til it found another way in.

This was an older fear. One built on a different man, grayer, thinner but somehow still possessed of the same smile. A grin composed more of rictus than mirth.

She'd been what, seven? Eight years old maybe, riding the

bus home, the sun winking in the windows through a break in the trees. She'd been in her red coat, her favorite, the big puffy one with its pockets stuffed with candy and stickers and rocks and dried up leaves. Her She-Ra backpack between her knees, laughing with her best friend Tina over...something.

Cupcakes! That was it! It had been a classmate's birthday. The laughter and giddiness of a sugar high, their energy boundless while it lasted.

She'd hopped off the bus still laughing so hard she didn't notice no one was waiting for her until the bus had rumbled away, gray exhaust trailing behind like it was a fat, slow missile.

She'd stood on the sidewalk, head turning every which way, unsure what to do, even though home was only four houses down. Someone always met her when she got off the bus. Most times it was her mom, smile on her face, cigarette held loosely at her side. If not mom then Grampa or Grandma, but never nobody. She remembered the sidewalk being empty, not even a squirrel moving in the trees.

She'd stood there, feet shuffling, for several minutes before finally setting off for home. As the wind whipped her ponytail from one shoulder to the next, she kept expecting to hear her name called or the honk of a car horn.

But no sound came.

Just beyond the hedges that marked the edge of their property, she got another surprise. Daddy's car, his big wood-paneled station wagon, was parked in the drive.

Daddy was never home this early. He never walked in the door 'til she and mom were about to sit down to dinner. She tried to think why he might be home. Her thoughts turned to a surprise, but her birthday was forever away, so that couldn't be it. Finally, she resolved to stop thinking and just be happy Daddy was home early. She skipped up the drive, still at the age when it never occurred to her that something might be wrong.

She wasn't old enough to have her own key, so she was forced to knock on her own door, a fact the sugar in her blood found hilarious.

Mommy came to the door, her face pale, a tissue in one hand and she choked when she saw Claire. "Oh baby! I'm so sorry! I forgot to meet you at the corner."

"S'okay."

"Are you okay, sweetie? Were you scared? Did anything happen?" Mommy pulled her inside and started to smooth out her ponytail.

"Yep. Nope. Nuh uh," Claire said, turning in a circle.

"Good, good. I'm glad. Did you have a nice day at school?"

"Where's Daddy?"

Mommy hesitated. "He's in the den sweetie, but right now isn't—"

Claire was off before Mommy could grab her. "Daddy? Daddy?"

"Claire! Claire, wait! Leave Daddy be, sweetie."

"Daddy?" Claire's legs carried her down the hall like a car on bald tires. She careened off a doorframe without slowing and took the corner in a hairpin turn, sneakers screeching.

She found him on the far end of the couch, near the big sliding glass backdoor. He was dressed in a brown suit, and the orange-gold light of late afternoon turned him hazelish from head to toe.

"Daddy!" she squealed, grinning from ear to ear. She threw her arms up high, ready to be plucked off the ground like he was a giant bird flying her off to far away mountains.

But the game never started. Her feet stayed rooted to the floor, while her mouth fell open.

"Sweetie," her mother ran in behind her, hands coming to rest on her shoulders. "Daddy's not feeling well. How about you come into the kitchen with me? You can help me make dinner and tell me about your day."

"Daddy, are you okay?"

Her father turned his face more into the light. His features disappeared in the glare, but she watched him wipe a hand across his eyes. "Daddy's fine, baby."

She was too young to understand how the word 'broken' could be applied to people. Or how anyone could smile even though they were miserable. All she knew was that her Daddy's face was awful and there were tears in his eyes, making them glint like ugly marbles in the light.

"How's my pretty girl today?"

Claire pressed herself back against Mommy, pulled Mommy's hands tight around her. Fear and panic rose in her chest, built to a high keening she couldn't keep from blaring out. Daddy was *wrong*. And wrong things were supposed to belong to strangers and midnight monsters, not on your parent's faces in the middle of the day.

It was a whole forever before she finally calmed enough to go near him, though looking back, it couldn't have been more than a few minutes. Time stretches, becomes interminable for a child frightened not by, but *of* her parents. Before then, she'd never noticed the gray in Daddy's hair, the streaks like filaments in a busted light bulb.

It wasn't until she was in high school that they finally told her the truth. Daddy's older brother, her uncle John, dead of an aneurism that very morning. The poor man had been driving home when it hit, and though no one else was hurt, he'd still been gone before the car finally crashed to a halt.

Without Uncle John, daddy struggled for months to keep their furniture business from going under, which was a good way to describe the man himself, in fact. Going under. Even now, decades later, it was hard to think of her father without the

droop of his head or the wrinkles pulled taut even when he smiled.

Eventually, with Mommy's help, he moved on and put the wrongness behind him. They never let Claire see how close they came to losing everything. All she ever saw of it were their drawn and weary looks.

Claire shook her head, thrashing at the memories as though they were crows pecking at the harvest. Turning her head slightly, she listened to Mike moving about in the next room.

*It must be a Flannery woman quality*, she thought to herself. Falling for men who refused to be mended until they were falling apart.

Closing her eyes, Claire mentally steeled herself. The next year...shit, the next few months would be hell. But she wasn't inexperienced at this. She'd seen it before. She could be the one to do the mending now.


Later that night, Claire lay awake and regarded her husband with worry.

Mike was a side sleeper. He never spent more than a few seconds on his back. Just flopped from one side to the other like a quesadilla on a flat-top.

But tonight was different and Claire's skin tightened at the sight.

He was as taut and coiled as she'd ever seen him. His knees were tucked close to his chest, one arm wrapped almost protectively around his head, and he moaned quietly, plaintively as if he were taking a beating in his sleep.

Her heart sickened as she watched, the weight of it a heavier burden than Gabriel could ever be.

Carefully, gently, Claire reached out and stroked his arm. His skin was flushed and hot, but she used her fingers like a cool, damp cloth. A balm that worked its way through one swipe at a time. It took half a minute but finally his arm uncurled, and she could see his face past a fold in his T-shirt. In the weak light coming through the windows, many details were lost, but the beset-upon look she found was enough to suck her lower lip between her teeth.

Sliding closer, Claire kept up the slow sweep of her fingers, even though she was afraid it would wake him at any moment.

She brushed his hair and ran the back of her hand across his cheek. She rubbed his chest and his thighs and over the course of several minutes he relaxed.

His knees came down, his face cleared. His breathing became less forceful and strained. Claire smiled but as his legs stretched out further, she noticed a shadow that instantly grabbed her attention.

She hadn't meant for her touch to be sexual, but from the way the front of Mike's sweats tented...Claire shook her head. Men were so simple sometimes.

As she looked at her husband's dreaming face, a new thought formed. She grinned.

Around his hips there was a small bit of space, a long stretch of skin lay between T-shirt and sweats barely an inch wide.

With the same gentle caress, she widened the gap slowly 'til her nails could scratch along his stomach, 'til she could run her palm up into the thick hairs of his chest.

She could feel his heartbeat pounding, an excited, tympanic vibration that rolled up her arm. He rumbled as she dragged her fingers down to the waistband of his sweats. She put pressure behind her touch, knowing it would wake him but also knowing this was something he needed.

"Mmm-Love?" Mike's eyes fluttered and Claire almost laughed. His body was ready before he was even conscious.

She kissed the tip of his nose, smelling their minty toothpaste on his breath. "Hush, Babe."

Two quick tugs and the drawstring on his sweats came loose. He stirred as she tugged them open.

"Love, what are you—?"

She pulled away his boxers and tucked her hand in, took hold of him.

He gasped and trembled slightly. She drew her hands along the underside of his shaft and his mouth opened. The deep draw of his breath caused a warm tingle to skirt low in Claire's belly.

Tucking her head in, she kissed him, his lips barely moving as she continued playing with him.

"Love," he said, as his hands mangled the pillow. "You, uhhh. You don't have to..."

"Shhh." With her free hand she tried to pull his sweats lower, but he stayed where he was. His cheeks were full of creases from the pillow. His hands inched across the sheets as though hindered. As if he were fighting himself, and now was not the time to ask him why.

She wrapped her fingers around him and stroked slowly, steadily.

"God." He grabbed her shoulder tight. Slid his hand down to her breast and caressed it even as he shook his head. "The doctor. The doctor said not to."

"Hush, now." she said, and finally he gave way. Mike lifted his hips and let her shuck his sweats down to his knees with a sigh.

The air leaving his lips had a ring of relief to it. Claire kissed him again. A thank you for not fighting her anymore.

The position was an odd one though. She couldn't put him on his back; the beach ball that was her son a hurdle she couldn't leap over. Instead, she slithered down the mattress, mentally thankful Mike talked her out of getting the other bed she'd wanted when they were first married. The one with the great big footboard.

With her feet hanging in midair, she tucked a hand under her head. Her mouth was on a level with him, the beat of his heart bouncing him like a needle on a scratched record.

Claire pushed his pants and boxers down all the way then tossed them to the floor. She dragged her hands up his calves to his thighs, each individual muscle responding to her touch. The skin of his balls tightened under her warm breath. He smelled of cotton and soap and that sharp man's scent he gave off whenever they got close like this.

Claire loved that scent: a musky, virile smell that would stay on her skin for hours. Pressed there by his weight, infused into her by the wild power of his hips as he let go. As she brought him to her lips, the weeks since they last made love were there, every hour and day and there was no better moment to make up for all of it.

He slid along her tongue the way he always did. Smoothly, with a twitching need. The taste of him woke up a hunger within her: the saltiness as she licked the underside of the crown; the sweetness as she took him in by inches. With every slow glide of her lips, he groaned. His hips quickly matched her rhythm in a giving, taking, retreating, returning movement set to gasps and moans.

In minutes, a new taste spread across her tongue, a potent earthy liquid that trickled from him. Claire pulled back a moment, saw the wet shine she'd painted across him. In the low light, her tongue darted out and caught the bit of spider silk which stretched from lip to tip. Reeling it in, she moaned and dove back for more.

She threw herself into the rhythm, her mouth leaping ahead, leaving his hips to catch up. She loved the slick feel of him. Reveled in the little twitches as she took him deep. Relished the way he jerked as she lathed her tongue around the tip of him.

"Claire. Oh God."

His fingers found their way into her hair. They roved through, bunched whole handfuls into his fists as his hips began to lose control.

Claire pulled back again and kissed the length of him. She reached up and cupped his balls, rolled and massaged them gently as she stroked him in a furious rhythm.

"God!"

She could feel him closing in. His legs were shaking, his breath came in great gusts.

"*Claire.*"

At the moment his body started to spasm she took him again. Her free hand swept round and clutched his bare ass. Drew him forward and took as much of him as she could, 'til tears welled, and her breath was cut short.

He didn't cry out. All she heard from him were strange clicks and wheezes and a resounding silence, but his body shouted for him.

It shuddered and convulsed, bowed and pumped and pumped and pumped 'til her need for breath overrode all other pleasures.

She smiled as she wiped her mouth. He continued to give as her fingers stroked him. Bits and pieces, white and pearlescent, spattered onto the sheets even as he softened. The quaking slowly subsided, his body at last coming to rest as one long powerful sigh walked away from him.

His hands slipped from her hair, allowing her to shimmy back up the bed.

Claire smiled as she felt a tiny kick, wondered if she'd woken the boy while putting the man to bed. She slid a comforting hand around the globe of her belly and hummed a quiet, wordless tune. The kick did not repeat. Claire opened her arms and Mike snuggled sleepily against her.

The push of his body rolled her until she was almost on her back. His head nestled against her shoulder, one arm snaking just under her breasts.

The position hurt like hell. Between his weight and that of Gabriel, it felt like her internal organs were being compressed by a thirty-pound stone that just happened to have very sharp elbows.

And yet, despite the pain, Claire remained where she was. She knew she'd never be able to fall asleep like this and in ten minutes she'd have to heave herself up to go pee anyway. But Mike's cheeks were slack, his eyes no longer tensely shut.

Her boys were asleep.

Though she knew tomorrow would come too quickly, she held onto the quiet as fiercely as if it were a lifeline. There was peace here in the room with them. A peace they'd needed for a long, long time and as Claire closed her eyes, she silently prayed.

*Let it be enough, Lord. Please, let it be enough.*

They called him in at ten. His hackles rose even before he had put the phone back in the cradle. It was little more than a week 'til the office closed.

Before those damn rocks could try to bury him again, Mike sucked in a big lungful of air and thought about that morning. Waking up next to Claire, the warmth of her pressed against him. The steady roll of her breathing, the smell of her hair, the fact that his pants were somewhere on the floor by the foot of the bed.

*God.*

The memories nearly had him ready to go again and though he hated to turn them aside, right then wasn't the time.

Mike stood at his desk. He rolled his shoulders and gripped that good feeling as tight as he could. He straightened his tie and stepped out into the main office, Claire's solid words about their future helping to put some steel in his step.

Cubicles took up the entire center of the floor. A long rectangle three desks wide and ten deep with the visitor's area just off to the left. The room was occupied by dozens of different conversations along with the clicking of keys, ringing phones, the whirr of printers and scanners ringing like a cracked bell.

Down a short hallway to his right he could just make out the kitchen and Tom's office door which was locked and for all the choice words he could use for the man, he had to admit it was a rare occurrence. Tom almost never took a sick day. It was one of the attributes management liked about him, for all his bluster and short temper. Mike tried to catch Alma's eye as he passed, but she had a phone squeezed between ear and shoulder, both hands practically glued to the keyboard. He forced himself to shrug it off and kept his head high, shoulders square as he rounded the corner.

Pat's office door was wide open and the moment he looked up, Mike wanted to dive back around the corner. Christine was with him. The chief of human resources. Mike couldn't think of even three occurrences where he'd run into her over the last year. She was the type of manager only ever heard from through other people.

*Christine wants this done by close of business Friday.*

*Christine needs that report retyped.*

*Christine decided to change where we're having the holiday lunch this year.*

Mike's instincts were firing on all cylinders, but he didn't dare stop walking. He could only pray the fear didn't show on his face.

He entered the office and sat down without waiting to be asked. Pat had his 'I have news' face on, but Mike couldn't read anything from Christine. She wore a bland, lukewarm smile Mike imagined would work well for weddings or funerals.

"Hi, Mike. It's good to see you again." She didn't offer to shake hands.

"Nice to see you too," he said.

Pat bobbed his head and cleared his throat. "Well, Mike we'd uh...like to talk to you about the final transition for the offices next week." His eyes flicked to Christine, and Mike was unsure why he even bothered to speak. It was clear from her body language that she was in control of this meeting.

She inclined her head in what Mike figured was meant to be a conciliatory gesture. "We know the normal work around here never stops but there is still a lot to be done before we officially move. Packing files, arranging transportation for furniture, lighting a fire under Telecommunications to port over the phones."

She chuckled as though it were funny, and Mike worked up a smile for it too. Pat laughed longer than he needed to and fell silent again.

"Given everything left to do, plus setting up the new office," Christine pressed on, "we're going to need someone to coordinate on both ends. So..."

Mike's chest burned. His vision was blurry, and a painful roar was growing in the back of his head. It took him a moment to realize he'd stopped breathing. He took a deep, slow breath, and fixed his attention on that meaningless smile.

"We'd like you to pick a team of coworkers, eight in all. No need to run the names by us, we trust your judgement. Just coordinate everything from here and get it done on time. We want as smooth a transition as possible before we re-open."

She left it there and leaned back. Crossed one knee over the other, like she expected it to take a minute for him to see the forest for the trees. And to tell the truth, he did.

Right then, he forgot everything. Forgot that he hated these two faux people, these half human beings. He forgot about the insane commute and the long hours and a son on the way because the *relief* flowing through him was so powerful it burned all else away like an incendiary grenade. He was so suddenly and deliriously happy it was a fight not to cry.

Over the next few minutes, they filled him in on the details. He'd finally be a supervisor. Ten thousand more a year and that was just to start. It also meant longer hours, more work and about a dozen additional layers of bullshit, but he didn't care. It meant safety and security and the kind of breathing room he'd been needing.

Over and over again, he shook their hands. He laughed at

jokes he never heard and all the while his dad's face superimposed over theirs. That smile. That proud, elated smile that said he'd made it.

Ten minutes later, on the way back to his desk, he'd already made the decision. He wasn't going to call Claire. He couldn't just ring her up and tell her they really *were* going to be okay. The phone possessed too much distance. Too impersonal.

He needed to walk in the door with a smile on his face. Flowers, dinner from their favorite restaurant, dessert, 'the whole ten' as dad used to say. He'd pull her to him, feel his son kicking happily away and lay it all out. God, he could already see the look on her face.

The rest of the day trudged by like it had weights in its shoes, but none of it was hard, not hard at all. He scheduled team meetings and organized files on the people he would pick, his selections coming to mind with barely a thought. Lauren couldn't come with them, that much was obvious. She was dead weight at best and a hindrance at worst. And as for Tom...Mike's good mood was such that a momentary twinge of sympathy flared for the man, but it wasn't long before it was quickly and brutally smothered. Tom had been heaping abuse onto him for months on end. If Mike even so much as thought about taking him on, he might as well shoot himself now.

With a definitive stroke, he dropped the files into Patrick's mailbox and set about the rest of his day, but even then, his fingers wouldn't cease twitching. Every time they reached out to the phone; his hands would tense like hunting dogs. They'd hang there immobile and say, *Please, please, please, let us go. We've got a job to do.*

Towards the end he made different calls. The florist, then Toscana's for their Mozzarella en Carozza, house salads, bread with homemade ricotta and Linguine Nerre. Mike's mouth watered at the thought of shrimp, scallops, octopus and mussels. Then, to top it all off, a pair of huge chocolate covered cannolis filled to the brim with homemade cream.

Even the snow didn't bother him, coming down as thick and fast as it was. The snowflakes were the size of paintball pellets, peppering the ground at his feet, but what did it matter? So it added another thirty minutes or even an hour to his commute. He'd be home all the same. With Claire and Gabriel and a new lease on life.

Only when he was behind the wheel, seatbelt fastened and the car carrying him home, did he remember his briefcase. Still upstairs, under his desk.

The thought flitted through his mind like a leaf over a field. It couldn't have mattered less to him, because his brain wasn't even in the car anymore. It was miles down the road at the florist, the restaurant, and in his own living room wrapped up in the arms of his wife as her laughter vibrated against his skin.

The night flew by in a steady whistle, and he chuckled quietly to himself. The snow did take its time and made the landscape unfamiliar. But still.

Mike drove and laughed.

The cold surprised Claire by how not-monstrous it was.

She walked out the backdoor expecting to be reminded of how bad an idea this was. But to tell the truth, it wasn't as cold as it'd been all week. Granted, when the temp has to struggle to break into double digits, that's not saying much.

Claire was as bundled up as she could get, the space between scarf and hat so slight everything above and below her nose was in a kind of No-Man's Land. She didn't come out here often, but she could only stay cooped up for so long before needing to get something other than carpet and linoleum under her feet.

The snow was already calf-deep and if the weather-guessers were right, they would all see their kneecaps disappear before morning. But right then, Claire didn't care about the next day.

She stood still for a minute, letting the flakes patter softly against her. Closing her eyes, she thought of sitting beneath the big bay window in the house she grew up in, wedged into the couch in her footie pajamas with a picture book in her lap.

She would try reading for a time but then, without looking, her little fingers would find their way back to the lamp behind her. A quick twist of the knob, and the shadows would drape about her like a blanket.

Storms were her favorite things to watch, snow particularly. It always brought the best of things with it, like snow days and snowball fights. She and her father had tried for years to build a snowman but never finished. It always devolved into the two of them laughing and running around, flinging snowballs at each other while a four-foot headless lump sat dejectedly in the corner of the yard.

She'd fallen asleep to snowstorms who knew how many times. Lulled by the quiet, relentless snow.

Tonight, though a snowman was out of the question, Claire smiled and imagined what building one with a ten-year-old *boy* would be like. She looked forward to chasing Gabriel around their own headless lump.

There might not have been much of a wind, but with each passing minute, the trees bowed more and more under the growing weight of the snow. Even stepping carefully, Claire could still feel the slip of the ice beneath. Smirking, she shook her head. Mike would not be happy if he found her out here.

Claire had never known him to be a yeller but coming home to find his about-to-pop wife frolicking around in a snowstorm might be just the thing to have him shouting the neighborhood down.

Even though it was a risk, the sight of the snow and the pull of her aching butt were too strong. She needed to get up and move about, if only to remind herself she still had legs.

The smell of the snow blanketed everything except the sharpest smells. Wood-burning fires, cigarette smoke, gas powered snow blowers. And while their backyard had little in the way of wandering space, Claire only needed to make a few crunching tours. Enough to wear away the slick feel of confinement on her skin. On her third and final circuit, she stopped at the edge of the garden and cleared away a bit of snow with her boot.

Through a plume of steamy breath, she smiled. It wasn't always easy for her to remember. At times her emotions were less like a part of her and more like hammers she regularly took beatings from. But on rare occasions she remembered Mike's words. About there being another spring with fruits and vegetables and a baby gibberishing away.

Leaning in closely, Claire studied the handmade signs as though she might divine what sort of veggie lover her kid would grow to be. Tomatoes? No, too acidic. Zucchini? No, too tough. Cucumber! Yes, that felt right! Clean and crunchy. Gabriel would be her Little Cucumber and Claire grinned maniacally at the thought of tormenting him with the name for years to come.

Laughing under her breath, she continued to scan the signs. The basil would need a little help at first. But once it was up on its feet, they'd end up with more than they could use. The dill and scallions, on the other hand, practically took over the garden in the last years. She'd have to be careful this time around.

Inwardly, Claire warmed at the thought of picking fresh mint leaves again.

Deep in the rows, practically flush with the fence, was another sign—one she couldn't quite make out. This one was parsley, wasn't it? Or was it sage? Claire stepped closer and crouched but though the light wasn't terrible, she still couldn't make it out. She blinked but that did nothing. The sign refused to come into focus.

Closing her eyes Claire rubbed them hard, but when she opened them again, even the signs closest to her faded in and out. It was like the blurriness which comes from standing up too fast. Except instead of clearing, Claire's head swam harder the longer she looked.

The signs became jumbled, and colors collided. Breathing heavily, Claire took a step back and nearly fell. Her right leg threatened to buckle, and her right hand was nothing but a mass of pins-and-needles. Keening softly, she wrapped her arms around herself trying to get a grip.

Something was wrong. Wrong in an essential way, like how a worm will shrivel up an apple from the inside, implacably eating away. Putting all her weight on one leg, Claire fought the snapping beat of her heart and the weakness pervading her limbs.

Blinking, she shook her head hard and gasped as the snowflakes blurred into long white streamers. The trees were sopped up by the storm, becoming lost in the wind.

Dread sunk its fingers into her like the grip of a stranger out of a crowd. Her jaw ached, her skin felt feverish, and everything was...Claire blinked and found herself facing the house. Shaking and sweating all at once, she stared at the open back door but had no memory of ever turning around.

She breathed shallowly and staggered towards the door,

towards the soft light bleeding out into the storm. The house was maybe twenty steps away, but she was so tired, so cold and hot and weak and scared. She needed help. She needed Mike. She needed someone to pull her in out of the frost.

Claire threw herself forward awkwardly. Her right leg was numb, and her left leg was trembling. She swayed heavily, moving in a *swish-clomp, swish-clomp* hobble.

She made it four steps. Then five. The screened door lurched in its frame even as she made for it.

Six steps. Seven. Her mouth filled with a cold, sick taste, like the slush kicked up by the passing plows.

Eight steps. Nine.

She hugged her good hand around her stomach. Gabriel kicked even faster than her heart.

Ten steps. Elev—

The pain overwhelmed her like a blow to the back of the head.

Falling to her knees, Claire bawled and shook. She rifled her fingers through her hair as though searching for the crude tools that were hacking and gouging away. Her skull felt ready to cave in. Shrieking sparks of pain bloomed and she mewled helplessly. Inside, Gabriel quaked, and her heart broke for him. His fear and pain were as palpable as her own.

Claire yearned to cry for help. To scream for someone to come and save her *son*. But all she could do was fall. Listing to one side, she crashed to the ground, still shaking. The house with its warmth and its light beckoned her on but soon even this began to fade. Her vision narrowed down and down, the edges becoming nothing but a shifting grey and white film. It swallowed the house, the garden, the light and all her promises 'til there was nothing left.

Nothing but the snow.

Mike hopped out of the truck like he owned the world. Dinner was clutched under one arm, roses in the other and he loved the crunch of snow under his heels as he walked up the drive. It took careful maneuvering, but he managed to fish his keys out of his pocket without dropping anything. The lock clicked and he shouldered his way in.

"Hello!" he called, off balance and laughing. "I'm home!"

Kicking the door shut, he swung into the kitchen and deposited dinner onto the table. The sweet smell of tomato sauce and fresh seafood trickled down his throat.

"Hey, Babe! C'mere, I've got something for you!"

The flowers swung gently in his hand. That no answer came surprised him but didn't slow him down. He turned the corner headed towards the bedroom. At the sight of the closed door, he slowed, lightened his steps. His fingers wrapped around the knob, and he heard the tiny *skrit* of the wood as he poked his head in.

Nothing.

The bed was empty, the sheets not even rumpled.

He glanced over his shoulder but the bathroom at the other end of the hall was half open and dark. He shifted his feet and the scent of the roses drifted to him cloyingly. Somehow not as lovely as it had been a minute ago.

The light was on in the office, the chair facing out as if Claire had just stepped away. At the foot of the stairs, with his hand on the rail, he thought about checking the attic. Was actually three steps up before he stopped himself. The house was so small, his voice would have traveled through it like a heartbeat.

Back in the kitchen, he picked up the box with dinner and set it on the counter. She'd probably left him a note about where she'd gone. As he rifled through the junk mail, bills and supermarket receipts, a thought jabbed him.

*Where would she go on a night like this?*

No note, no message. His stomach filled with a growing unease. It sloshed as he stood there, instantly souring the little that was left from lunch. Mike licked his dry lips and listened as the two sides of his head went to war.

*Maybe she went out with a friend? Somebody could have picked her up.*

*None of her friends live close by. She would have told you she was leaving.*

*Maybe she went for a walk? Needed something. The store isn't far.*

*It's the middle of winter.*

*Maybe...*

*She would have called!*

Mike pulled out his phone, cursed and then dropped the useless thing on the table. Grabbing the cordless, his fingers skittered over the keys. He pressed it to his ear, the worry traveling from his stomach into his lungs.

*Ring.*

His arm swung unconsciously, beating the flowers against his leg again and again. Petals flew across the floor.

*Ring.*

She was out with a friend. Had to be. It was just baby brain. She'd just forgotten to—

*Ring.*

That time he heard it. A second, muted ringing, like an echo. He swiveled his head. Cocked it to the side and concentrated.

*Ring.*

The door at the back of the kitchen was open. An echo

drifted through it along with a frigid breeze that touched his skin like cold fingers.

"Claire!" he called. Putting the cordless down, he listened carefully. *"Claire!"*

Nothing.

Mike took two lumbering steps and then was flat out running. He never stopped to open the screen door, just plowed through, ripping it off its hinges.

The second he was outside he nearly lost his footing, but he didn't care. Only what was near the garden mattered. Claire's parka, as red as a cherry, lay on its side half buried in the snow.

Mike's brain couldn't make sense of it. His eyes would light upon the parka and the cap and the scarf, but his thoughts scattered in panic, fleeing even as the rest of him ran closer.

Dropping to his knees he stared at Claire's boots, painted in dusty white. They existed separate from the coat because what connected them couldn't possibly be what Mike was seeing. Those weren't Claire's legs, splayed wide, or her fingers hooked as though grasping something Mike couldn't see. And those weren't Claire's eyes staring out, lifeless and unblinking at the ever falling...

All feeling left him. It drained out in a rush like blood leaving an open wound. He lost the cold of the snow against his knees, the scratch of Claire's coat in his hands, even the frantic pounding of his heart. From close by a scream pealed across the yard. Long and hoarse and tortured. For Mike it was the worst sound he had ever heard in his life.

"Do you have anyone you can call?"

Dr. Larson was Claire's OB. The hospital called him once the ambulance pulled into the ER. He was a short man with fleshy cheeks and a thick stubble. He was dressed monochromatically from head to toe. Black slacks, white shirt, black tie, white socks. He simultaneously sat beside Mike while keeping as far away as he could physically get.

Mike was dressed as if winter had walked in with him, arm in arm. Heavy, down coat buttoned and zipped up to his chin, gloves and cap pulled on tight. He'd even thrown the hood of his coat up over his cap, but still he shook. The nurse who took him back to Larson's small, windowless office had asked if he wanted her to take his coat, but he said no, teeth chattering.

"Your wife's file didn't list any other emergency contacts. Do you have someone who can drive you home?"

St. Joe's smelled like nothing at all. He'd been inside Larson's office dozens of times and always there was that telltale hospital smell. Industrial strength cleaning products and sickness, the funk that came from people sweating, fretting, going home and never leaving. But the smell was absent as if it had never existed. And it wasn't the only thing missing.

"Mr. Harper...Mike. I'm very sorry for your loss. If you want, we can put you up here at the hospital for the night. Have a car drive you home in the morning..."

Mike closed his eyes and tapped a heel against the floor. Listening carefully, he did it again, but the sound was deadened somehow. Like it had been made by a different man in a separate room.

"We believe she had an aneurism, based on how she was found. It may have caused a stroke, but there's just no way to be sure without an autopsy. Given her body temperature when the paramedics brought her in, I'm afraid she was out there for some time."

Mike opened his eyes and jerked when he saw Larson. He'd honestly forgotten the man was there.

"Mike," said the doctor, a look of discomfort on his face. "I realize this is difficult, but unfortunately with the amount of time and the weather, there was just no way to save them. I'm terribly sorry."

"Terribly," Mike said flatly. His voice sounded abused, as if he'd been screaming for weeks.

"I can't imagine what..." Larson coughed. "I know this is a lot to take in, but it would be highly beneficial if you would give us your consent for an autopsy. It would help us determine what happened to your wife and would clear up any—"

"That's the fourth time you've said 'would' in less than ten seconds."

"Mike." Larson was sweating. His mouth hung open and his hands never stopped moving. "I know you may...you *are* under a lot of—"

As Larson went on, Mike tucked his gloved hands under his arms and squeezed hard. He curled forward and tried to breathe slowly. His stomach hurt in an unnatural way. Like he'd taken a beating he couldn't remember.

"Mike? Mike, are you listening?"

Claire used to sit like this. Eyes closed, arms wrapped around herself. Only she'd be turning green and telling Mike how she'd changed her mind. *He* could be the one to carry the kid. She was done.

"Have...Have you heard anything I've said?"

Mike looked up. "I can't feel this chair."

Larson shook his head as if Mike had just hit him in the face. "What?"

"The chair. The one I'm sitting in right now. I can't feel it." Mike ran his hands along the molded plastic arms and his head cleared all at once. Gripped by the power of a sudden, obvious thought. "This isn't really happening, is it?"

Larson reached out. "I think you're in shock."

He put a hand on Mike's arm. But the hand was so *cold*

Mike trembled and slapped it away. The doctor's face flickered in and out like the reception on a rabbit-ear television.

"I-I think I need to leave."

"I really can't recommend that. You're in shock. Why don't we go to the—"

"I need to leave." Mike's stomach worsened. It constricted hard, fighting him but he wouldn't listen. He planted his feet.

"Mike, you're in no condition to go anywhere."

"I can't. I can't feel..." Mike heaved himself up, groaning through clenched teeth. He couldn't stand up straight. His stomach was like a wound threatening to open. His head pounded and his mouth was dry. "I need. Can't."

"Mike please, you need to listen to me. I'm going to call the nurse and we'll—"

The pain left him in a torrent. It exploded out of his mouth, splattering against Larson's tie in brown, green, yellow and black.

"Ahhh!" The doctor leapt backwards, furiously wiping at his ruined shirtfront.

Mike stood swaying. Strings of pain hung from his chin, and he tasted sour apples though he couldn't remember eating any. Larson was bent over double, both hands clamped over his mouth, his skin a stricken pale. Mike tried to apologize but his whole body was crumpling as if someone clipped him right in the knees.

He heard a shout, saw a nurse come running around the corner. Falling forward, vision fading in and out, Mike's teeth chattered, and his limbs no longer obeyed him. Unmoored and unprotected, he couldn't even scream.

It broke off in his throat the moment his head struck the floor.

Friday January 22, 2016

Tom couldn't move without pain.

He couldn't even sit still without a sharp constant ache, like someone was digging a screwdriver into his leg. He sat behind his desk and did nothing but breathe deep and slow, fighting not to think about the things he should have been doing. Like running the Encounters Report, helping customers and digging through old files. Hell, by now he should've already cracked the whip on his team, made sure they weren't fucking up too badly. But he couldn't do it. He didn't have the energy or the time and even if he did, it wouldn't matter.

By day's end they wouldn't be his team anymore.

Pat didn't even have the guts to tell him on his own. He brought in Christine from HR. They took him into the conference room and sat him down all nice and friendly. Made sure to keep themselves between him and the door. Like they expected him to lose his fucking mind and murder them.

And he *would* have. No bullshit about that. But every time he twitched his fingers, the splints would rasp, jabbing needles of pain into his arm. If he so much as swiveled in his seat, the Velcro boot smacked against a table leg.

It muzzled his anger, crippled every curse that wanted to charge across his tongue. In the end, when they asked him to finish out the day cause golly-gee-fucking-willickers, Mike hadn't made it in yet, he couldn't so much as growl. Just nod while choking on an ice-cold rock in his chest.

Once he got back to his desk, he let his head drop and rubbed his eyes. *Okay troop. What now?*

He was a sixty-one-year-old gimp who couldn't walk up a flight of stairs without running short of breath. Not a day went by that didn't see him hack up something wet and brown. The house was still years away from being paid off and even if the fucks had kept him on, his salary wouldn't have left him much to live on. Not now that he was paying for everything himself. There wasn't much of a nest egg to speak of, and the company insurance would run out by the end of the month.

Tom fought to shrug his shoulders. He'd started over with less. He could do it again.

*You right about that, troop. But back then you didn't have as many years on you.* Tom sat up straight and felt his stomach bump against the edge of his desk.

*You never had this much weight on you either. But don't you worry, troop. It'll be okay. Medicare may be a few years away but you can see the Poor-House from here.*

Tom stood up so suddenly his chair crashed against the wall. Coffee. That was the name of the day. Something to keep him sharp. Fuck the team, fuck the reports and fuck everything else. Coffee was all that mattered.

Face scrunched against the pain, he limped out of his office, heads lifted as he passed, and he stared down each and every one of them until they returned to their work. Only Alma, her arms loaded with files, said anything to him.

"Hey Tom, you doing okay? You need anything?"

"Coffee."

"Ha! That's funny. I was just thinking of making a run. Give me a minute and I'll—"

"*I'm* getting coffee. I don't need *you* to make a special trip for me."

Alma's face looked like it was performing a vertical pincer movement. The eyebrows and forehead attacked from the north while the mouth and chin mounted an assault from the south.

"Sorry I offered." She said it like she wanted to gnaw off his fingers.

She stomped away and Tom told himself not to dwell on whatever the hell she was thinking. Get the coffee, get back to the desk. Make some calls. Light a fire under your contact's asses, if they'll even pick up the phone. It wasn't much of a plan, but he'd managed more with less, so it was a good place to start.

---

The cab lurched and skidded as it made its way down the road. With one hand pressed against his stomach, Mike gripped the *Oh Shit* handle and tried to lean with the car.

He'd overheard nurses say that plows and sand trucks had been out in force all night, but Mike would never know it from the white-gray state of the roads. It was full of ice patches, ruts and potholes that shook the frame of the car every few seconds, no matter how much the driver fought to avoid them. They laid in wait like trolls, ready to rattle Mike's teeth whenever he let his mind wander.

"Saw the governor on News 12 last night. The *governor*," the cabbie said, a sixtyish, potbellied man with a bushy, unkempt gray beard. He gripped the wheel hard in both hands, the stub of an unlit cigar pinned between finger and assembly line rubber. "He was standin' out there in this three-piece suit prob'ly cost as much as this car. You should've seen 'im! He had this sour look on his face, like he usually sends his aide out to deal with the weather, but the kid banged in sick."

The cabbie guffawed and slapped the wheel.

"And then...And then you know what he says?"

Mike hadn't uttered one single word since the orderlies wheeled him over to the cab.

"He says there's gonna be a three hundred dollar fine for anybody on the roads after eleven o'clock! What? They're gonna fine people for being stupid, now? Jesus! If you're gonna do that you should start with the people that voted for ya, jackass!"

Despite the ridiculous temperature, Mike cracked the

window, hoping the air would save him from the stench of the cab. It was soaked in an overheated, moldy mishmash of smoke, body odor and carelessness.

The cabbie's mouth kept flapping, but Mike's attention drifted away. They were rolling up to the intersection of Hempstead and Wantagh, the snow on the roads so thick the traffic lines were invisible.

Off to the right, a snowplow was doing donuts in the Pathmark parking lot, its giant, concave snout creating drifts that climbed twelve feet up the lamp posts.

Every tree Mike saw was encased in ice. The bare branches whipped crazily in the heavy winds like natural wind chimes. He could hear the clinking and tinkling even over the driver's wheezing laugh.

Though he couldn't see the traffic light from the backseat, he felt the crunch of the wheels as the cab gouged its way to a halt. When it started jerking in place, Mike worried that the transmission might be going. But a quick glance up front proved it to be an impatient foot having an on-and-off again affair with the brake. Less than a minute later, the light changed, and the relationship ended. They'd just started creeping into the turn when a loud, angry honking stopped them dead.

Mike jerked forward in his seat, the strap biting into his shoulder like a feral child. Out in front of them a silver SUV, horn wailing, flew wildly into the intersection. Mike craned his neck and glimpsed the driver, a woman with glasses and a cell phone cranking into a turn that would have been idiotic under normal weather conditions.

Brakes shrieked, tires squealed, and her car slammed into the curb so hard it was like a heavy-bag getting hit by a sledgehammer. Two wheels lifted clear of the ground and for a long heartbeat it just hung there. The woman's mouth was fearful wide, a scream ready to go as the car tilted...tilted...tilted...Then, with an almost mournful creak, it crashed back onto all four wheels. Mike flinched as the woman's head connected with the doorframe.

They were window to window with cars honking on all sides. The woman sat very still, her teeth gritted, and one hand pressed against her temple. When she took it away Mike couldn't see any blood, but a welt was already forming. She slowly shook her head but made no move to look in Mike's direction.

With the exaggerated care that comes from sudden death and near misses, she put down her cell phone and adjusted her ponytail. Seconds later, her primping complete, the entire intersection watched as she drove away, puttering as cautiously as an octogenarian traversing a flight of stairs.

The cab driver laughed his ass off all the way to Mike's door.


Once away from the main roads, the snow was purer. The gray-brown slush hadn't worked its way into the residential streets yet. Cars lined both sides of Silver Street, bricked in up to their door handles by the plows.

Though it was early and still snowing, here and there people were out, their backs put to shovels or hunched over snow blowers. As the cab rolled along, geysers of white launched into the air from sidewalks and the bottoms of driveways.

By the time they turned onto Balsam, the driver's laugh had become a wet hack. He alternately pounded his chest and shook his head, the edge of his smile reflected in the windshield. Mike thought he sounded like St. Nicholas after a three-day bender.

*That's a good one. Claire would like it. I'll have to remember to tell her when I get—*

The driveway was buried. He couldn't even see the edges.

The surface of his lawn was so brilliantly white it hurt to look at it. Turning away, Mike studied the great big block of snow piled high on the roof of the Explorer.

Absently, he wondered what would happen if he opened the garage. Would the snow come avalanching in and take him out at the knees? Or would it just stay there, perfectly formed like graham cracker crumbs in a pie plate?

The driver threw one hairy arm over the seat and shook his head. "Jesus, that's a helluva thing to come home to. You need any help gettin' to the door? I can wait for you if you want to just grab some stuff, you know. There's a Hilton not too far from here."

Reaching into his pocket, Mike pulled out a handful of bills and held them out. The driver looked at him for a second but then just shrugged. Mike's fingers were white and had split in places from the cold. Dried blood stained at least two knuckles, but he hardly noticed. He kicked the door open and left the cabbie quietly counting to himself, a cigar stub lodged firmly in one corner of his mouth.

With his bag of belongings, meds and discharge papers, Mike trudged up the drive, nearly losing his shoes twice before he got to the door.

The act of coming home was so habitual, he moved without thought, throwing open the door before he could give himself a chance to prepare.

The normalcy caught him off guard.

A perfect warmth, the kind he'd been looking for since winter began, greeted him just inside the door. Claire's TV tray was in the same place as always, the lights still on and he could almost *hear* her voice calling to him from the kitchen. Could imagine her coming around the corner, lips formed for a kiss.

He waited there 'til his feet screamed at him.

Mike dropped the hospital bag and slumped onto the stairs.

His head, a ridiculously heavy thing, landed in his hands with a thud. He coughed hard, his stomach twisting, but there was nothing to come up. He hadn't eaten in hours, but it didn't stop his muscles from bunching. The pressure convulsed him, pushed all the air out of his lungs and squeezed him 'til he couldn't see, couldn't hear...

He curled up into a ball on the landing, his mind blank. There were so many thoughts rocketing around at once it was like a white noise.

Finally, what got him moving wasn't any conscious will of his own. It was the slight feel of resistance against his heel, a quiet crinkling of plastic when his leg kicked out.

Mike coughed thickly and sat up. He'd forgotten about the bag and his kick had sent it skittering across the rug, half gutted of its contents.

On his knees, and for no other reason than because it required no thought, he picked up the bag and hollowed it out fully. Meds rolled across the floor. His scarf, wrapped in plastic, hit with a dull *thwap*. He could still smell the sick through the covering, a scent his brain processed as green and black. He flung the scarf away and almost did the same to the paperwork, but at the last second, he stopped himself.

There were two dozen important looking forms and he grabbed one out of the pile because...he didn't really know. Because his hand was calling the shots. Because it was the only yellow one of the bunch. Because why the hell not.

*Disposition of Effects* it read, in bold, black, double underlined letters. Underneath it was *St. Joe's* and some chicken scratch that was probably a doctor's signature.

For a long minute, Mike didn't understand why they'd given this to him. A check of his pockets proved he'd come home with everything he'd taken with him. Keys, wallet, clothes, busted phone. It was all there. Yet he continued to stare at the yellow paper, his overclocked brain turning the word 'effects' over and over again, searching for coherence.

Down at the bottom, Claire's name was typed out straight and neat just above yesterday's date and beside it a was signature line with Mike's own name printed and *Oh my God, Sweet Christ, please no.*

Mike's hands trembled so badly they tore the paper in two, rendering Claire's neat little name. Hurling the pieces behind him he reached for the other pages, his breath ragged, his head whipping back and forth. He clawed past a glossy pamphlet on how to deal with the loss of a loved one. Crumpled a listing for grief counselors and suicide hotlines.

But the *Request for Autopsy* form drew out a whimper that nearly broke him in half.

It was all filled out for him. All it lacked was his signature. He stared at it and the longer it went on the more a sound grew in his head. It was as loud as a church bell or a scream, but it was the exact same words over and over again.

*You left them. You're here and they're still there. You left your wife and son behind!*

Mike crab-crawled across the carpet and ripped the end table drawers out of their tracks. He dug through bills, instruction manuals and laptop chargers. Growling, he bashed his knuckles against the top and slammed it closed.

"The fuck is it?!"

It wasn't 'til he was back in the living room, feet leaving dirty treads all over the important papers, that he remembered. His briefcase. He'd left it at the office.

Mike had so many people to call. Their lawyer, the hospital, their friends. But his phone was fucked and the only other place he kept those numbers was in his briefcase.

Mike made a sound like he just pulled a pigsticker out of his gut. He dug his nails into his palms and beat his fists against his thighs. Leaning over, he reached for his wallet and almost crashed to the floor like a drunk on a tear. Righting himself he staggered for the door but stopped with his hand on the knob. *What do I say to them?*

He never called in, never so much as phoned to say he would be late. He'd have to walk by all those eyes, bear the brunt of questions from a dozen mouths.

*How am I doing, Sarah? Oh, I'm just fine. Why didn't I call in, Alma? Well, you see, I broke my phone. Yeah, did a real good job of it too. Busted to Hell and back again. No Pat, I'm sorry. I'm afraid I can't stay to work my shift. Why? Well, that's a great question.*

"I have to pick up my wife and son."

It was barely a whisper, but it was the loudest thing in the house. Mike unlocked the deadbolt and threw open the door. It took ten minutes to clear off the truck. Another hour to shovel the drive enough for him to get out. Tires spun, snow and ice flew but he made it. Out in the street, even the road fought him. It grabbed at his tires, tried to pull them from his grasp. The wind pitched the snow almost sideways, but he wouldn't be stopped. He drove through it all, his lips silently forming the same words over and over again all the way through the storm.

---

Tom clenched his fists to keep from reaching out and steadying himself against the wall. The itch was in his throat again, scratching, scratching, scratching against him, looking to turn his lungs inside out and scrape them clean. He swallowed jerkily every few seconds, counting the steps back from the kitchen. He was almost to his office when he saw Asshole Mike lurching ungainly through the office, nearly bowling him over.

"Well hey, look who it is!" Tom crowed. "Finally decided to come in, asshole? Well we're awful fucking glad to see you."

Mike said nothing and tried to brush past him. Tom wobbled into his path. "Was the snow too bad for you? Was that what kept you away from us? Well, it wasn't so bad for the rest of us, buddy. But I guess you needed a day off after *stealing another man's job right out from under him!*"

Mike looked like he'd slept in his clothes in the back of somebody else's car. He was nothing but wrinkles and uncombed hair. There was dried gunk in the corners of his mouth and a smell of vomit stuck to him like he'd bathed in it. Tom crinkled his nose in disgust.

"Jesus Christ! If you're gonna go out and live it up at least have the decency not to look like shit the next day!"

Still not a word. Not a sound. Mike wore a look Tom had seen before. His mouth hung open and his eyes were so glazed over they may as well have been opaque. Even standing still he looked almost as unsteady as Tom himself.

"What happened, Mikey? Did you enlist and get sent into combat in the last twenty-four hours? Or did the party go south on you real quick?"

Cowardly little fuck couldn't even look him in the eye. He just stared blankly down the hall. Tom stuck his face in real close and smiled.

"Look pal. I know there's a whole room full of people around the corner ready to kiss your ass. But let me be the first to say...*Fuck you!* Do you have any idea what I'm gonna have to do now? Or where I'm gonna fuckin' be?"

A bubble of drool popped on Mike's lips as he mumbled something.

"What?"

"I have to pick up my wife and son."

Tom shook his head and blinked. "That's not...Why are you

even...*I don't give a fuck what you have to do!* I'm out of a job because of you, you little bitch! You owe me more than just— Hey! Where the fuck are you going?"

Mike had shaken him off and kept moving.

"I have to go. Claire. Gabriel. They're waiting for me."

Tom sneered. "Yeah, I heard you the first time. Well I wouldn't worry too much. I'm sure they're used to you fucking up. Just like the rest of us. Don't leave 'em out in the cold too long, Mikey! They might not be there when you get back."

He watched Mike march off down the hall and gritted his teeth. He wanted to spit but hobbled back to his office instead. Fuck it. He'd get coffee later. Once inside, he kicked his garbage pail with the wrong foot. There wasn't anything in it but the contact hunched him over, grimacing.

"Fuck! Fuckin...shit. Swear to fuckin' God, they are gonna wish..."

His office door clicked shut behind him. Tom turned.

"Mikey? What the fuck? Did you forget about the wife and kid alrea—"

The punch caught him right in the temple. The world went sideways, and he staggered.

The next one hit him square in the teeth, snapping his head back. He felt a tooth come loose and he tasted blood. Mike collided with him, driving him back into his desk.

Instincts long out of use kicked in at last. Tom tucked his chin and barely managed to get his hands up in time to block the next blow.

"Wait! Mike, *please!* Hel—"

An elbow slammed into his jaw. Another drove deep into his gut. Mike never stopped swinging and the look on his face...*Holy Christ.*

His eyes were bloodshot and manic. His teeth gnashed and spittle flew as he fought like an animal driven mad from wounds and hunger. He was pure fury, and it was almost enough to make Tom piss himself.

He fought as hard as he could, taking blows to the ribs and the side of the head, trying to wrap Mike up, to fend him off long enough to run for his life. But Tom's lungs were scorched, and his heart pounded wildly. He couldn't draw a full breath and his head felt warped, like one good blow would knock it clear off its moorings. When Mike growled in his face, the first warm dribbles of piss ran down his leg.

Finally, Mike threw a wild left and Tom lucked out. Stepping into it, he wrapped Mike's arm up with his own and locked it against his side. A right came screaming towards his throat but he blocked it and held on. Sweating and shaking, Tom strained to build up some leverage—to at least spin Mike away from the door. But the other man's foot came down on his shattered toes and a bloody, raw wail broke free of him.

Reeling in agony, he tried to recover but his mangled foot slid out from under him, and he toppled. The back of his head cracked against the filing cabinet and what little fight he still had bled away.

He landed between the wall and his desk, his good arm trapped beneath him, legs tangled. His head throbbed and his gorge rose dangerously high, the taste of blood and meds caustically sweet in the back of his throat.

"Pl...ple. Mi-ike. Please. Mike, I'm so—"

A heavy weight landed on top of him, chased all the air out of his lungs. Mike's face was blurry, almost surreal, but his hands as they closed around Tom's throat were as solid as all the years behind him.

Tom bucked and thrashed but the tight space and Mike's weight kept him pinned. He struggled but the best he could do was free his broken hand. He swung, but without leverage the splints rebounded off Mike's shoulders.

He pawed at Mike's grip, tattered memories of how to apply a thumb lock floating in his head. His ears filled with the roar of his heart and little black spots erupted in his vision. Between them, through them, something loomed. It had all the makings of a face but there was nothing human in it. Just rage and hate and blood and teeth.

The black spots expanded, became so big they had a gravity to them. There was no breath, no thought, just the pull and Tom was almost glad for it. He never wanted to see that face again. Never wanted to be this scared or hurt ever again. Not like this.

Please.

---

Mike squeezed until he thought his thumbs would snap. His wrists, arms, shoulders, even his back, it was all one long aching line.

Tears filled Tom's eyes and the frantic, machine gun fire of his pulse pounded against Mike's palms. His lips kept trying to form words, but all Mike could hear were the little clicks and squeaks of air fighting to escape.

Tom's face was bright purple, and his tongue protruded wetly between his lips. Mike stared down at him, his head full of nothing.

No, that wasn't true. His thoughts were a long way off, but he wasn't completely empty. There was still a feeling. One hard to describe.

It was like he was back at the scene of that accident. Only this time he wasn't speeding through, terrified he was about to plow a man down. He wasn't even himself really. He was outside, standing on the side of the road gazing at the broken glass and sizzling road flares, hearing the screech of his brakes.

He was there for all of it, but now, from outside looking in, the horror fascinated him.

There would be no escape. No thread-the-needle slide between. It would all end badly but he didn't want it to stop. He had gone too far for that now.

Tom's windpipe gave with a wet *crack* Mike felt rather than heard. Tom's chest sank as though deflating and bloody spittle gurgled past stilled lips. Mike almost let go of him then but a flicker deep in Tom's eyes stopped him.

Something was there and Mike leaned down even further to be near it. His tongue tingled to life and his stomach groaned with hunger. Hunger for something big and encompassing and awful and—

*Dear God.*

Mike stared at Tom's eyes in wonder. The hard mocking brown he had grown so used to was all but gone, pushed to the thinnest edge by angry, blood red vines and a cold, hollow center. The other man's pupils had taken on a depth and weight, as though they were glimpses into a black well Tom was silently falling through, the last few pieces of him beckoning for Mike to follow.

Mesmerized by all that red and black, Mike found himself calling up memories he no longer wanted. Claire lying on her side buried in white, her dead eyes gazing upon a barren garden. Gabriel. The son he'd seen only in pictures and scratchings. The boy he would never hold or kiss or watch grow up.

Then there were all the years he'd spent lashed to a desk, working far too hard for people he hated. The clients who treated him as less than human. The friends who disappeared when he needed them most.

Mike scooped up all of those memories and threw them down the well by the handful. He hurled them as hard as he could while beneath him, Tom's last struggles bled away. He settled slowly into the floor and though Mike kept his grip tight, he knew it was over. The well was closing up, the vines withering away.

Seconds passed with no sound, just the vibration of Mike's heart in his ears, and though he breathed heavily, there was a strange lightness in him as he climbed slowly to his feet. He couldn't open his hands, the muscles protested violently, and his back popped and crackled as he straightened but...

He took a deep breath, so deep that his lungs might've gone on forever if he tried. The smells of dust, furniture polish and shit hung around him, but Mike drew it all in without a cough or a ripple.

He waited for the feeling to pass but it didn't, instead something else took its place, or more like a lack of something. As if he were suddenly less than he'd been just a minute ago.

Standing there swaying, Mike thought of everything he had thrown down into the red and black, all those fears and hatreds. They'd been a part of him for so long they were more like old friends than anything else, people he'd grown up with but no longer knew how to talk to anymore. They were gone now, all of them, and would not be missed, though they'd taken something else with them, something essential, only marked by its absence.

Deep in his bones, Mike wondered what it was, but 'empty' was all that came to him. He was empty now, scraped clean of everything, but it was an emptiness he thought he could live with.

Closing his eyes, Mike started to take another forever breath when a stunned gasp forced him to turn.

Patrick stood in the doorway, coffee mug gripped in one hand, his face afflicted. His lips trembled and his eyes skipped about, going from Mike to Tom to the bits and pieces they'd destroyed in their wake. Tom's computer lay on the floor by Mike's feet, a perfect shoeprint smashed into its screen. Papers were torn, books scattered, and blood dappled every cheap surface.

Patrick looked at Mike's hands, the fingers still hooked, knuckles scraped raw and bleeding. He shivered but made no move to run. Those wide, panicked eyes finally returned to Mike's face and a terrified whine dribbled across the debris.

"M-Mike? Are—"

"Yes, Patrick?"

His boss recoiled instantly, and Mike shook his head. There was something wrong with his voice, too scoured and pitted and...Calm.

"Are..." Patrick tried again. "Mike, are...Oh my God, Mike. *Are you okay?*"

The quiet was awful, but what followed was worse.

Mike started to laugh.

He laughed hard enough to double him over. Loud enough that it filled the room before pouring out into the office beyond. It ripped Mike's throat apart, painting his teeth red but couldn't be stopped.

Patrick paled and a dark stain spread down one leg. With the awful thing roaring in his head, Mike wanted to take him by the arm and tell him yes. Yes, he really *was* okay now.

But each time he tried, the words only fed the laughter. Stoked it 'til it grew in volume and reformed into an ear-splitting cackle. Patrick's heels slapped against the floor as he ran away screaming that Tom was dead and there was a maniac just down the hall.

Mike watched him go, wishing he could run after him. There was so much still to be said, so much Patrick needed to hear, but his lungs finally ran dry, and his knees buckled. As he sank to the floor, everything he had fought for and lost crashed together in his head like boats caught in a storm and all at once Mike realized he was happy to see Patrick go. Happy to stay right where he was and laugh and laugh 'til the whole world ran out of breath.

Because way down at the bottom, beneath the pain and the loss, the laughter and the freezing cold waves swallowing it all, he knew one thing.

Patrick would never get the joke anyway.

# ACKNOWLEDGEMENTS

This book, as well as its author, has been on a long and very strange road. I started writing it almost a decade ago, before I even knew what genre it was in. All I knew then was that it dealt with my nightmares, and I needed to get it out or go mad.

After all these years, I am indebted to a number of people for their help and encouragement. Without them, I probably would have stopped pushing for it long ago.

First up, I have to thank my mom for instilling in me a love of reading and for always believing I would make it as a writer some day. Love you, Momma. I have to thank my dad for his encouragement and imagination and for teaching me that getting lost isn't always a bad thing. Thanks must go to my wife for always looking out for me, and to my daughter just because she's awesome, hands down. Thank you to Pam, my friend who taught me how to talk and how to save my own life.

Thanks to Lisabet Sarai, Belinda LaPage, Adrienne and all the others at ERWA who saw this book in its early drafts and gave me a way of making it better. It still tickles me that a horror story got its teeth sharpened in erotica.

A special thank you to Sam at Bowler Fern, my first editor on this novel. Without Sam, this book wouldn't have been nearly as good as it is. Another thank you to Laurence (and all the folks at Darkstroke), for giving me the opportunity. And finally, thank you to Betsy and Bloodhound Books.

Getting to this point wasn't easy, but thanks to all of these people I, and this story, have been able to see the light of day. I will forever be grateful.

# ABOUT THE AUTHOR

Henry Corrigan is a bestselling author, husband, father, and bisexual creative who dreams of writing every kind of story. His debut novel, *A Man In Pieces*, won the Silver Medal from Literary Titan and was shortlisted for the Top 25 Indie Books of the Year. His horror poem, *The Litany*, was featured in <u>SHARDS</u>, a mental health charity anthology from Ravens Quoth Press (2024) and his queer haunted house novella, *Somewhere Quiet, Full of Light*, is due out from Slashic Horror Press in 2026. Always an avid horror fan, the first book Henry ever stole was a copy of Stephen King's Night Shift. (His mother eventually stole it back.) He is a member of the Horror Writers Association and the admin for the Horror Writers Collaborative on Facebook.

As an obsessive, overly anxious person living with depression, he has dedicated himself to providing readers with the diverse, flawed characters that he desperately needed when he was growing up. Above all, Henry wants to be known for not staying where he's been put. To always surprise people, especially himself. Because that's what makes it fun. The feeling that even he doesn't know what he's going to do next.

9 781917 214551